"Go home, Daron."

She stood there in the rain, looking at him with dark eyes. "When it stops raining, I'll fix the roof."

"I'm not going anywhere. You have a sick little girl in there. Let me do this."

She put her fists on her hips. "If you're going up, so am I."

As she went for the ladder, he watched her, then averted his eyes, because looking too long just didn't seem right.

He'd gotten through the last few years by thinking of her as his friend's wife. But she wasn't anymore. He remembered Andy, how they'd talked about him being a dad. But he never did get to be a father…

"Stop, Daron," she said as if reading his mind. "Stop thinking about it or you'll never move past that day, the guilt. Let's make a deal. We'll be friends, the kind that help each other out because that's what friends do. Not because they feel guilty."

Friends. Yeah, they could be friends.

Who was he kidding? He wanted a lot more from Emma than friendship.

Brenda Minton lives in the Ozarks with her husband, children, cats, dogs and strays. She is a pastor's wife, Sunday-school teacher, coffee addict and sleep deprived. Not in that order. Her dream to be an author for Harlequin started somewhere in the pages of a romance novel about a young American woman stranded in a Spanish castle. Her dreams came true, and twenty-plus books later, she is an author hoping to inspire young girls to dream.

Books by Brenda Minton

Love Inspired

Martin's Crossing

A Rancher for Christmas
The Rancher Takes a Bride
The Rancher's Second Chance
The Rancher's First Love
Her Rancher Bodyguard
Her Guardian Rancher

Lone Star Cowboy League: Boys Ranch

The Rancher's Texas Match

Lone Star Cowboy League

A Reunion for the Rancher

Visit the Author Profile page at Harlequin.com for more titles.

Her Guardian Rancher

Brenda Minton

HARLEQUIN® LOVE INSPIRED®

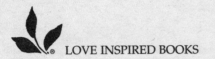

LOVE INSPIRED BOOKS

Recycling programs for this product may not exist in your area.

ISBN-13: 978-0-373-89904-3

Her Guardian Rancher

www.Harlequin.com

Printed in U.S.A.

Now faith is the substance of things hoped for, the evidence of things not seen.
—*Hebrews* 11:1

To the police officers and also to the men and women of the armed forces—because their constant sacrifice keeps our communities and our nation safe. May we show them respect and continue to uplift them in our prayers.

Chapter One

The moonless sky was dark and heavy with clouds and a promise of rain that would be welcome, since most of November had been dry and December promised more of the same. Daron McKay eased his truck down the driveway of the Wilder Ranch, away from Boone Wilder's RV, where he frequently crashed on nights like this. Nights when sleep was as distant as Afghanistan, but the memories were close. Too close.

On nights like this he took a drive rather than pace restlessly. A year ago he would have woken Boone and the two of them would have talked. But Boone had recently married Kayla Stanford and the happy couple had built a house on the opposite side of the Wilder property.

Daron had his own place, a small ranch a

few miles outside of Martin's Crossing. He rarely stayed there. The house was too big. The space too open. He preferred the close confines of the camper. Not that he wanted to admit it, but he liked Boone's dog. He also didn't mind Boone's large and raucous family.

His own family was a little more restrained and not as large. And his appearance sometimes bothered his mom. He didn't shave often enough. He preferred jeans and boots to a suit. His dad, an attorney in Austin, wanted his son to join the family law firm rather than run the protection business he'd started with friends Boone Wilder and Lucy Palermo. His mom wanted him to attend functions at the club and find a nice girl to marry. His sister, Janette, was busy being exactly the person her parents wanted her to be. She was pretty, socially correct and finishing college.

Daron was still coming to terms with his tour of duty in Afghanistan, with the knowledge that he could lead friends into an ambush.

One of those friends had died. Andy Shaw had only been in Afghanistan a few months when Daron and Boone followed an Afghan kid who claimed his sister was in trouble. The sister. Daron pulled onto the highway, gripping the steering wheel, getting control of the memories. He'd thought he loved her, so when her brother came to him and said their family needed the help of the American soldiers, Daron had agreed to go.

He'd been young and stupid, and because of him, Andy had died. At thirty he didn't find it any easier to deal with than when he was twenty-six.

The truck tires hummed on the damp pavement. He headed his truck in the direction of Braswell, a small town in the heart of Texas Hill Country and just a short distance from Martin's Crossing. He cranked some country music on his stereo and rolled down the truck windows to let cool, damp air whip through the cab of the truck.

A few miles outside Braswell he turned right on a paved county road. He slowed as he neared the older farmhouse that sat just a hundred feet off the road. Only one light burned in the single-story home, the same light that was typically on when he made his midnight drives.

And he made this trip often. When he couldn't sleep. When he felt the need to just meander by and make sure everything looked okay. It always did.

But not tonight. Tonight a truck was pulled off the road on the opposite side as the farmhouse. The parking lights were on. There was no one inside. He cruised on by, resisting the urge to slam on the brakes. A few hundred feet past the house, he turned his truck, dimmed his headlights and headed back, pulling in behind the other truck and reaching in his glove compartment for his sidearm. Unfortunately it was locked in the gun cabinet at the trailer.

With quiet steps he headed toward the house, staying close to the fence, in the dark and the shadows. He kept an eye on the house, scanning the area for whoever it was who owned the abandoned truck. If it hadn't been idling, he might have thought it was just broken down and that the driver had decided to walk. But the engine running meant the driver planned to return fairly soon.

He was near the back of the house when he heard the front door slam open. He moved in close to the side of the house and rounded the corner and then he stopped. The front porch light was on and caught in its glare was a too-thin Pete Shaw with a ball bat swinging in his direction. The younger brother of Andy Shaw jumped back quick, avoiding the aim of the woman advancing on him.

"Get out. And don't come back. Next time I'll have more for you than this baseball bat,

Pete. Stay away from my house. Stay away from my family. We don't have anything."

Pete lunged at her, but she swung, hitting his arm with the bat. He let out a scream. "You broke my arm!"

"I don't think so. But next time I might." She raised the bat again. She might be barely five feet tall, but she packed quite a punch. Daron resisted the urge to laugh. Instead he took a few quiet steps forward, in case she needed him.

"I'm not going to let you hit me, Emma."

"You're not coming back inside this house." Emma Shaw swung again and Pete fell back a pace, still holding his injured left arm.

It looked as if he planned to leave. Daron remained in the shadows, watching, waiting and hoping Pete would walk away. When the other man lunged, Daron stepped out of the shadows. "Pete, I think you ought to listen to her."

Pete turned, still holding his left arm, still looking kind of wild-eyed. He was thin. His hair was scraggly. Meth. It was easy to spot an addict. The jerk of the chin. The jumpiness. The sores. A person couldn't put poison in his body and expect it to be good for him.

"This isn't your fight, Daron." Pete held

up his right hand, showing he still had half a brain. "But I'll make it your fight."

Or maybe he didn't have half a brain. Andy's younger brother took a few steps in Daron's direction.

"Really, Pete?" Daron remained where he stood. "Get in your truck and get out of here. Get in a program and get some help."

"I don't need help. I just need the money. I know she's got it hid somewhere."

"I don't have money, Pete. I don't have anything but bills. You blew through the money Andy left. You bought that truck and you bought drugs."

"None of us were at the wedding," Pete countered. "I doubt you were even married to my brother."

"Go away, Pete. Before I call the police." Emma advanced on the other man, as if she were taller than her five-foot-nothing height. Daron stepped forward, coming between her and danger.

"Pete, you should go." Daron said it calmly, glancing back at the woman who didn't appear to be in the mood to appreciate his interference. He wasn't surprised. For three years she'd been telling him to go back to his life, that they weren't his responsibility.

Pete backed away, his eyes wild as he

looked from one to the other of them. "Yeah, I'm leaving. But I'll be back. I want what belongs to my family."

"Go. Away," Daron repeated.

He followed the other man to the road and watched him get in his truck and speed off into the night. When he returned to the house, Emma was gone and the front porch light was off. He grinned a little at her bravado and knocked on the door anyway.

He didn't mind that she kept up walls with him on the outside. It certainly hadn't kept him from watching over them. Them meaning Emma, her aging grandfather and the little girl, Jamie. Even with their limited contact he was starting to think of her as a friend.

A friend who didn't mind closing the door in his face. He grinned as he lifted his hand to knock a second time.

Emma leaned against the door, needing the firm wood panel to hold her up. Her legs still shook with fear and adrenaline. She'd barely gotten to sleep when she heard a window opening, the creaking sound alerting the dog that slept on the foot of her bed. Fortunately her grandfather and Jamie had slept through the racket.

Racket? No, not really that drastic. She'd

pounced on Pete as he climbed through the window. He'd pushed back, hitting her into the china cabinet, but she'd steadied it and herself, managing to get a good grip on the baseball bat she'd carried from her room.

Pete wasn't healthy and it had been easy to back him out of the house and take control. Or at least it had felt like she was in charge. She'd had it handled.

The last thing she needed was Daron McKay in her home and in her business. But there he'd been, standing in the shadows like some avenging superhero, ready to rescue her.

He'd been playing the role of guardian since he got home from Afghanistan. He'd been at the hospital when she had Jamie. He'd brought gifts and food in the years since her daughter's birth.

No matter what she said or did, she couldn't convince him she didn't need his help. They were making it. She, Jamie and Granddad. They'd always made it and they would continue to do so.

Yes, it would have been nice to have Andy's help. But Andy was gone. No use crying over what couldn't be changed.

The door behind her vibrated with a pounding fist knocking just about where her shoulders touched the wood. She jumped back, letting out an unfortunate squeal.

"I know you're there," Daron called out, his voice muffled through the thick wood.

She didn't move, didn't speak. Surely he would take the hint and go away.

"I want to check and make sure everything is okay. And I'm not going anywhere until we know Pete isn't coming back."

Pete might return. She should have thought of that. Of course he would return. Usually he came during the day, demanding money she didn't have. Andy had divorced her just prior to deploying and he'd made Pete his one and only beneficiary.

She'd called him after he deployed, to tell him he was going to be a dad. He'd made promises about the two of them and she'd told him they could talk when he got home, not when he was thousands of miles away and she was still hurt by his betrayal and him walking away from their marriage. Slowly, hesitantly, she touched the lock, took a deep breath and opened the door. Her gaze slid up, her eyes locking with the gray eyes of the man standing on her front porch. Drat, but the man made her feel safe. As much as he annoyed her. As much as she wanted him to go away.

"Well, you opened the door." His voice was low and rumbled, sliding over her, causing goose bumps to go up her arms. She hugged herself tight, her hand touching a spot on her opposite arm and feeling a sticky dampness.

"Ouch." She glanced down. Her hand came away stained with blood.

"You're hurt. Did he do that?"

"I backed into the china cabinet. But I'm fine."

"We need to call 911 and let them look for him." He took her by the uninjured arm and started through the house with her, guiding her as if he knew the way.

"We don't need to call the police. He won't be back tonight. He's just a stupid, messed-up kid."

"A stupid, messed-up kid who's on drugs and breaking into homes. Let me look at your arm."

"I'm fine. You can go." Bravado didn't work when her voice shook, from fear, from aftershock.

"Let me take a look anyway. Even though we both know you're fine. Is this the first time he's broken in?"

She nodded as he led her into the kitchen. Without warning, his hands went to her waist and he lifted, setting her on the counter.

"Would you stop manhandling me?"

He grinned at that, as if he thought she didn't truly mean it, and he went about, rummaging through cabinets until he found salve and bandages. He wet a rag under the sink and returned. Without looking at her he took hold of her and wiped at the gash on her arm. She flinched and he held her steady, smiling a little but still not looking at her.

That gave her time to study his down-turned face, his eyelashes, the whiskers on his cheeks, the column of his throat.

She swallowed and tried to pull away. He glanced up then, his dark gray eyes studying her face so intently she felt a surge of heat in her already-flushed cheeks.

"How did you do this?" he asked as he dried the cut and then applied salve.

"I bumped into the china cabinet. Maybe I hit a rough edge."

"Maybe," he said. He opened the bandage and placed it over the wound. "It's pretty deep."

"I've had worse."

His hand slid from her arm and he moved, putting distance between them. His scent— country air, pine and something Oriental— drifted away as he backed against the opposite counter. She inhaled. Oh, and sandalwood.

No, she didn't want to notice his scent. Or his eyes. She didn't have time to notice him, to notice that she was female, still young and still willing to be attracted to a man like him.

"So this wasn't the first time he's been here?" he asked, his gaze intent, serious.

"No, it wasn't. He typically comes during the day. He likes to show up as I'm leaving Duke's." She'd started waitressing at Duke's No Bar and Grill last year, just to make ends meet. Between her tips and her grandfather's Social Security, they were making it.

Someday she'd finish her degree. She was taking classes online, and next year she would be finished and licensed to teach. Until then she did what she could. Breezy Martin, Jake Martin's wife, watched Jamie the few hours a day that she worked. She did her best to keep her daughter in an environment with few other children. It was important that Jamie stay healthy.

"You could get a restraining order," he suggested, still leaning against the counter. His arms were crossed over his chest.

"I don't want to do that. He was Andy's brother. Our marriage ended, but that doesn't mean I'm angry or that I want to cause problems."

"He's causing you problems." He brushed a

hand through his unruly hair, the light brown color streaked with blond from the sun.

"He's causing himself problems. He's an addict. My getting a restraining order won't cure him of that. His parents would use it against me. I took one son and I'd be taking the other."

"Took their son? You didn't take Andy." He glanced away. "I did."

"He volunteered for service in Afghanistan because he wanted to get away from me. If not for our divorce, he would still be here."

He opened his mouth to speak but then shook his head. "You're wrong."

She shrugged, unsure of what to say to that. She guessed she knew she was wrong. But right or wrong didn't change anything. Andy was gone. Jamie would never know her father. A family had lost their son.

"Neither of us can go back," she finally said. Because she thought they both wrestled with the past. Why else had he been driving by at this hour?

"No," he agreed. "We can't."

They stood there for several long minutes, the only sound the ticking of the clock and the hum of the refrigerator. He cleared his throat and moved away from the counter.

"I have to go. Will you be okay?"

"Of course I'll be okay."

Wasn't she always?

As she walked with him to the front door, she thought about the ten-year-old girl who had lost both parents and had been sent to live with a grandfather she barely knew. On the drive to Houston he'd repeatedly glanced at her and asked if she was okay. Each time she'd nodded to assure him. But each time he refocused on the road she would shut her eyes tight to hide the tears.

After a while she had been okay. They'd moved from Houston to this house. She'd learned to be a farm girl from Braswell, wearing whatever her grandfather thought she needed. Usually jeans, scruffy farm boots and T-shirts.

She could look back now and realize that in time she'd been able to deal and she'd been happy.

Life wasn't perfect. God hadn't promised perfection. He'd promised to be with her, to give her strength and peace. She knew there were mountains looming in her near future. She also knew they would get through the tough times. They would survive.

She had to. There was no choice.

Daron stood on the front porch, tall and powerful, a man most women would want to lean on. Just moments ago, she'd been that woman, leaning into his strong arms.

Momentary weakness, she assured herself. For that very reason she managed an easy smile and thanked him for his help. The dismissal seemed to take him by surprise, but he recovered. He touched two fingers to his brow in a relaxed salute, stepped down from the porch and headed down the road to his truck. She watched him leave, then stepped back inside and locked the door.

This time when she leaned against it, closing her eyes as a wave of exhaustion rolled over her, she knew he wouldn't be coming back.

Chapter Two

The next few days were uneventful and Emma appreciated the calm that followed Pete's midnight visit. Each morning she fed the cattle with her granddad, then headed to Martin's Crossing to Duke's No Bar and Grill to work the lunch shift as a waitress. Lately she'd managed a few extra shifts, which would come in handy with Christmas just around the corner.

She'd only known the Martin family by name before taking the job at Duke's. The last six months or so, she'd come to appreciate their family. Not only had Duke Martin given her a job, inexperienced as she was, but his sister-in-law, Breezy, had offered to watch Jamie.

Lily, Duke's daughter, swept into the restaurant on Wednesday afternoon, a big smile on her young face. Emma responded with a smile and a wave. The teenager followed Emma to the waitress station.

"Breezy has Jamie across the street at my mom's shop. She said she'll bring her over in a minute. She thinks maybe Jamie isn't feeling good."

Emma's heart sped up a little at that information. They'd been blessed this winter. So far they'd avoided major viruses. That was the goal. And a good reason for having Jamie at Breezy's, with fewer children around to spread germs. The twin nieces that Jake had gained custody of after his own twin sister's death were now in preschool. Jake and Breezy had a one-year-old who stayed at home with Breezy.

She recovered, fighting off the moment of panic. "Is she running a fever?"

"Breezy said she isn't. Mom thought she felt warm."

"I'll check her when we get home." She maintained a smile, to make herself and Lily feel better.

Nedine, Ned for short, Duke's head waitress and right-hand woman, walked out of the kitchen carrying a tray. The older woman, tall and big-boned, had once explained she'd been named for her dad, Ned. He'd wanted a son but he'd been happy with a daughter.

The older waitress smiled at Duke's daughter and winked at Emma. "Lily, your daddy said to put you to work when you got here after school. I think you're going to be my bus girl this evening."

Lily saluted. "Will do, Ned. Hey, did the twin foals do okay over the weekend?"

Ned's face split open like sunshine. "They sure did. Prettiest little palominos I ever did see. You'll have to come out and take a look."

"I will!" Then Lily returned her full attention to Emma. "Did my mom tell you about the potluck at our church this Sunday?"

The girl reached for the big jug of ketchup and started refilling bottles alongside Emma. Before Emma could answer her, Duke entered the restaurant. He caught sight of his daughter and headed their way.

"Hair in a ponytail, please," Duke said as he gave her a hug.

Lily responded by digging in her pocket and pulling out a hair band. She pulled her dark hair back in a messy bun and kept working.

"She did tell me," Emma answered the girl's question.

"Are you going to be there? I know you go to church in Braswell, but, you know…"

Emma nodded. "Yes, I know. You have someone you want me to meet."

"Kind of," Lily admitted. "He's nice. He works for my dad."

"I'm sure he's nice, but I really don't have time for dating." Emma blinked away a flash of an image. No! She would not think of Daron McKay and dating in the same thought. She wouldn't allow his image to startle her that way, coming unbidden to her mind, all concerned and caring the way he'd been last Sunday night. At least she knew it wasn't Daron who Lily had in mind for her. He didn't work for Duke.

"Are you okay?" Lily's shoulder bumped Emma's, nearly making her drop the ketchup bottle she held. "Oops, sorry. I didn't mean to scare you."

"You didn't scare me. And I'm fine." She pulled her phone out of her pocket. "It's a phone call, that's all."

Saved by the bell. She glanced at the caller ID and grimaced. An unknown caller. She didn't need that. It most likely meant it was Pete or a bill collector or something equally unpleasant. But when the caller left a message she lifted the phone to her ear to listen.

"Oh no," she whispered as she listened.

Lily stood next to her, eyes wide, ketchup bottle held close to her mouth. Emma took the ketchup bottle from the girl and set it on the counter before reaching into her apron for a pencil. She jotted down notes and ended the call.

"Is everything okay?" Lily, still wide-eyed, asked.

Duke came around the corner. "Lily, why don't you give Emma room to breathe? There are a couple of tables you can clear."

Lily moved away, reluctant, with slow steps and a few backward glances. Emma managed a quick smile for the girl before glancing up at her boss. He towered over her at six foot six. With his shaved head and his goatee, he used to intimidate her. Now she knew him to be a gentle soul.

"My grandfather seems to be in custody at the Braswell Police Station," she explained, still numb.

"I didn't know Braswell had a jail." Duke took the towel she was wringing the life out of and tossed it on the counter. "Is he okay?"

"Yes, I guess. He ran someone off the road. I guess I'll know more when I get there."

"Do you want me to give you a ride or find

someone to drive you?" His deep voice rumbled, reassuring her.

"No, I'm good."

"If you're sure. But call us later and let us know that you're okay."

Emma nodded, still in shock, as she headed out the diner.

The city police station of Braswell, Texas, was located on Main Street, between the Clip and Curl Salon and the Texas Hill Country Flea Palace, a fancy name for a store that sold everything from secondhand canning jars to old books. Emma parked her old truck in front of the police station and reached over to unlatch the car seat where her daughter, Jamie, dozed, thumb in mouth and blond curls tousled. Her eyes, blue and wide, opened as Emma worked the latch. She grinned around her thumb.

"Hey, kiddo, time to get up. We have to bust Granddad out of this place."

Jamie giggled, as if she understood. But at three, Jamie understood things like puppies, kittens and newborn calves. She didn't understand that her favorite person, other than her mommy, was getting older and maybe a little senile. She also didn't understand bills, the leaking roof or the desperate need to buy hay for winter, which was nipping at their heels in a big way.

The farm her grandfather had bought and moved them to when she'd lost her parents wasn't a big spread, not by Texas standards. The fifty acres had provided for them, though, supplementing her grandfather's small retirement. It had been a decent living until her grandfather's pension had gotten cut, and then they'd had medical bills after Jamie's birth. Emma had been forced to sell off most of her horses, all but a dozen head of cattle and get a part-time job. The economy and the drought had dealt them a blow the past few years.

All things work together for good, she kept telling herself. All things, even the bad, the difficult, the troubling.

Unbuckled, Jamie reached for Emma and wrapped sweet little arms around her neck. Emma grabbed her purse and reached to open the door of the truck. It was already open, though. Daron McKay was leaning against it, December wind blowing his unruly hair. His dark gray eyes zeroed in on Jamie and he unleashed one of those trademark smiles that might charm a woman, any woman besides Emma. Any woman who had time for romance. If her favorite top wasn't in the rag pile, stained with throw-up, and if her daily beauty routine consisted of more than a pony-tail holder and sunscreen, a woman might give Daron a second look.

But a woman going to bail her grandfather out of the city jail didn't have time for urban cowboys in expensive boots, driving expensive Ford trucks and wearing... Oh goodness, what was he wearing? It smelled like the cologne counter at the mall, something spicy and Oriental and outdoorsy, all at the same time. The kind of scent guaranteed to make a woman want to drop in and stay awhile.

No! She'd done this once before. She'd believed Andy, that he would help her, fix her life, make things all better. And he didn't. When things had gotten tough, he bailed. He hadn't been prepared for reality.

"Go away, Daron." Emma pushed past him with her daughter, because she was decidedly not the woman who wanted to lean into him and stay awhile. She didn't have time for anything other than reality.

Daron McKay was a nuisance and he'd been a nuisance for three years, since he got back from Afghanistan. He'd involved himself in her life because he'd come home and Andy hadn't. But Andy had left her long before then and Daron just didn't understand.

Andy had left her here alone.

Alone, broke and pregnant. Of the three she could handle alone. Other than with her granddad, Art Lewis, she'd been that way most of her life. Her parents had died in a car accident when she was ten. Art had been the only one willing to take her on.

Now, eighteen years later, the tables had turned, and she was taking care of her granddad.

"I can't go away." Daron followed her, reaching his arms to her daughter. Jamie, not knowing any better, went straight to him. He'd been hanging around for three years. Her daughter thought he was the best thing ever.

"Why can't you just go away?" she asked, knowing she shouldn't. "And how did you know?"

The wind, strong and from the north, whipped at her hair, blowing it across her face. She pushed it back with her hand and gave the man next to her, who towered over her by nearly a foot, an angry glare. Not because he was a bad person, but because he was always there. Always catching her at her worst, when she felt weak and vulnerable. He'd been in the waiting room the night Jamie was born. He'd been there when Jamie had the croup. He was always there. Like he thought they needed him.

He'd brought groceries, bought Christmas presents, provided hay for their cattle. He was kind. Or guilty. Maybe he was both. She didn't know and she really didn't have the time or energy to figure him out.

She did know he wasn't the least bit fazed by her attempt to push him away. "I heard the call on the scanner. And I can't go because I'm carrying Jamie. And she happens to think I'm amazing."

He smiled down at her and added a wink that made her roll her eyes.

"That makes two of you," Emma quipped, barely hiding a smile as she averted her gaze from the too-sure-of-himself rancher with his Texas drawl, sun-browned skin and sandy curls.

He laughed off the comment. "Yep, me and Jamie, we think I'm pretty amazing."

"It's time for you to cut the strings and realize I don't need you, Daron. I'm not your problem. You don't owe us anything. We're taking care of ourselves."

His smile faded and he glanced away, his gray eyes looking a lot like the clouds rolling over the horizon. "I'm here. Like it or not."

"I think you're upset that *you're* here instead of Andy. You are upset every time you take a breath. You have to let it go."

"He was a friend."

She looked at Jamie, then shook her head. "I'm not doing this again. We can't go back. I can't help you soothe your guilt. You have to let go."

"Your granddad ran a tractor off the road. He was fiddling with his stereo. He said they need to play more Merle and less of this stuff they call country these days. All of the good ones are dying off, he said."

Emma brushed a hand across her cheek, not wanting to think about the good ones dying off or songs about who would take their place. "I'll take care of it."

"There's damage to the tractor."

"Okay, thank you. You can go."

Daron remained next to her, matching his giant steps to her smaller ones. "Your granddad let his insurance lapse. It hasn't been paid in two months."

Emma sighed. "Could this get any better?"

It would get better, though. She knew in time they'd work through this. Jamie would be healthy and Emma would be able to work full-time. Things always got better. Sometimes they just had to get worse first.

"They mentioned having him evaluated."

Daron reached to open the door for her. "They think it's time he gave up his license."

"Of course they do. But he's only eighty and he's usually careful." She held her arms out to her daughter, but Jamie ignored her, preferring instead to rest her head on Daron's shoulder. "We have to go now, sweetie."

"I'll go in with you." He glanced down at the child in his arms, her blond curls framing her face. Put a hand to her cheek as if he knew the routine. "Is she sick?"

Emma briefly closed her eyes, because for a brief moment she'd forgotten what Lily told her. "She has a virus."

And then she took her daughter and walked through the open door, leaving him alone on the sidewalk. When she got to the desk where an officer was doing paperwork, Daron was still behind her.

"Can I help you?" The officer, his name tag told her his name was Benjamin Jacobs, looked past her to Daron.

"I'm Emma Shaw. My grandfather, Art Lewis…"

The officer grinned and held up a hand. "We know Art. He's in the back entertaining the guys with stories of the trouble he got into when he was overseas during the Korean

War. We'll get him processed and you can take him home."

He hit the intercom and told someone in the back that Art's granddaughter was there to get him.

"Do you have the name of the person he hit? I'm under the impression there are damages and Art's insurance has lapsed?"

"It's taken care of." The officer went on with his paperwork.

"It can't be taken care of. He doesn't have insurance. If you'll give me the name, I'll handle it. Or will we see them in court?"

"They didn't press charges."

She spun around to face Daron. He had taken a step back, but he was still close enough to poke a finger into his chest. "I said stop."

"Stop what?"

"How many times have I told you—you don't have to rescue us. We're fine."

He held both hands up in surrender. "I know you are."

A door behind them opened and closed with a click. She glanced back and saw her grandfather with the police chief. He'd lost weight and his overalls hung a little loose. He was wearing slippers instead of his farm boots. She drew in a breath, aching because he was getting older. Why had she thought he'd be with her forever, always picking up the pieces and keeping her safe?

"Granddad, what in the world?" She hiked her daughter up on her hip and closed the distance between herself and her grandfather. "Are you okay?"

He scratched the gray whiskers on his chin. "Well, I reckon I am. What are you here for?"

"I came to get you. They said you were in a wreck."

He tickled Jamie and smiled at Emma. "Oh, I wasn't in a wreck. It was a misunderstanding. I'm sorry for worrying you, kiddo."

"I'm..." She swallowed the argument because it would do no good. And she pushed aside her fear for her aging grandfather. "I'm sure it will be okay."

Jamie's arms tightened around her neck as a violent episode of coughing racked her small body. Emma buried her face in her daughter's hair, close to her ear, and whispered for her to take a slow breath. When she looked up, Daron watched with questions in his thick-lashed eyes. He towered over her, all broad-shouldered and strong, ready to help.

There were days when she wanted to give in and let him be the hero he wanted to be.

Not today. Today she wanted to go home,

help her child breathe a little easier and make sure her grandfather was okay.

"Is she okay?" Daron asked as she shifted Jamie to her other hip and pulled the hood of her jacket over her head.

"She's fine. And thank you. For being here."

"Emma, if you need anything…"

"I know."

She took her grandfather by the arm and walked him out of the police station. Daron didn't follow this time. She resisted the temptation to glance back, to see if he stood in the doorway watching.

Daron told himself to let it go. He knew that Emma was holding on to her pride by a thread that was coming unraveled fast. But he couldn't let it go. He couldn't watch her struggle to keep afloat knowing that he was partly responsible for her struggle.

Emma didn't want him in her life. He wanted to say he wasn't interested in being in her life. But he guessed if he was going to be honest, he'd admit that he was attached to her, to Art and to Jamie.

There was something about their little family. They didn't have much. He'd noticed a tarp on the roof, meaning it probably leaked.

Her truck tires were worn slick. They were content with that little farmhouse, the small plot of ground they owned and the few head of cattle they ran.

Content. He sighed. It had been a long time since he knew the meaning of the word.

From the window of the police station he watched as they all climbed into her truck. She leaned to buckle Jamie into the car seat. Art said something and she shook her head, but then smiled and touched his weathered cheek.

The cop said something to him about rain. Daron nodded and headed out the door. The cop had been right. The rain was coming down in sheets. He hunkered into his jacket as he hurried to his truck. Once inside he cranked the heat and turned the wipers on high. It was cold for December in Texas Hill Country.

He headed in the direction of Martin's Crossing, and the strip mall where he and his friends Lucy Palermo and Boone Wilder had their office. Since returning from Afghanistan the three had opened a bodyguard business. It kept them busy, supplying protection and security for politicians, businessmen and anyone else who might need and be able to afford their services.

Things had changed since Boone married Kayla Stanford, half sister of the Martins of Martin's Crossing. Boone was building a house. Daron was still crashing at the RV on the Wilder ranch.

Lucy remained the same. She was still a loner. She was still hiding things that might be buried deep, keeping her tied up in the past.

Daron was still reliving that moment when he saw his friend Andy die, caught in the blast of an IED. He remembered the face of the kid who had led them all, knowingly or unknowingly, into danger.

Just a week before that explosion, Andy had learned that Emma was pregnant. He'd shown all the guys the ultrasound picture of the baby, the tiny dot he'd claimed would be his son. Andy had divorced Emma, not realizing she was pregnant. And she'd let him go, he said, because she wouldn't force a guy to stay in her life.

Daron had made a promise to his dying friend that he'd check on Emma, make sure she and the baby were okay.

Daron had kept that promise. But after more than three years, maybe it was time to walk away.

Chapter Three

Emma came in from the barn on Thursday morning to find her granddad in the kitchen making up a cold remedy concoction that smelled a little bit like mint and a whole lot like something he'd cleaned out of the corral. He held the cup up, his grin a little lopsided beneath his shaggy mustache. His overalls, loose over an old cotton T-shirt, reminded her he'd lost weight recently. But he was still her granddad, her hero. She wanted him to live forever.

From the bedroom she could hear Jamie coughing. "I'm going to call the doctor."

Art pushed the cup into her hand. "Give her a sip of this. It'll help that cough."

She held the brew to her nose. "Art, what in the world is in this?"

"Mint to clear up her cough, some spices from the cabinet and a little cayenne."

"We can't give her this. She'll choke."

His mustache twitched. "It always worked for you."

"No, it didn't. I poured it out and then made a face so you would think it worked."

"And here I thought I'd invented a cold cure."

She set the cup down and gave him a tight hug. "You cured a lot of things, Granddad. Like loneliness and broken hearts. But you can't cure that cough. You can't cure her. And I know you want to."

His blue eyes watered. With a hand that trembled a bit more than it had a year ago, he pulled a white handkerchief from his pocket and wiped his nose. "I'd give this farm to cure her."

"I know you would. So would I." Emma brushed a hand down his arm, then turned her attention to the kitchen cabinet, intent on finding the right cough medicine and the inhaler that would clear her daughter's lungs.

But the asthma and the cold were the least of their problems.

The coughing started up again. She hurried down the hall to the room she shared with her daughter. The teenage posters of Emma's high school years had been taken off the walls and replaced with pictures of kittens and puppies. The twin beds were covered with quilts that Art's wife, a grandmother Emma had never known, had made.

Jamie was curled on her side, her blue eyes seeking Emma as she walked through the door. She'd seemed to be getting over this virus, but last night she'd taken a turn for the worse. Emma had known they would be seeing the doctor today.

"Hey, kiddo, need something for that cough?"

Jamie sniffled and rubbed her blanket against her face. Her cheeks were red and her eyes watery. Emma had given her something for the fever before she went out to the barn an hour ago. A hand to her daughter's forehead proved that this time a dose of over-the-counter fever reducer wasn't going to cut it. She leaned to kiss Jamie's cheek and managed a reassuring smile.

"We're going to get you dressed and take you to the doctor, okay?"

Jamie nodded and crawled into Emma's lap. Emma brushed a hand through the silky curls.

"Mama," Jamie cried, her voice weak.

"I know, honey. Sit up and take this medicine, and then I'll call Duke and tell him I won't be in today."

"Everything okay in here?" Art's gruff but tender voice called from the doorway.

Emma glanced back over her shoulder. "We're good. But we're going to take a drive in to town to see Dr. Ted. You want to go?"

"Nah, I'll stay here. But if you need anything, you call and I'll head to town straightaway."

"I'm sure we'll be fine. I think we just need something stronger than what I can buy at the pharmacy."

"That would be my guess." Her granddad stepped into the room, his smile tender for his great-granddaughter. "Ladybug, you need to get better so we can start learning to ride that pony of yours."

Jamie smiled a weak little smile, but her eyes lit up. "Blacky."

"Yeah, that's the one. He's a pretty little pony." Art brushed a hand through her hair. "Now, you be a good girl for your mommy and I'll make chicken noodle soup for you for dinner. They say that's a good cure for a cold. Better than my tea, I've been told."

Jamie grinned and the tension surrounding Emma's heart eased just a bit. "We'll be home soon, Art. Don't try to fix that tractor by yourself. We'll work on it together. If it has to wait until tomorrow, that's fine."

Art frowned. "Now, don't go getting sassy with me. I've been working on tractors since before you were born. I'm old, but I'm not feeble or ready for the rest home just yet."

"I agree, but there is no use getting hurt."

"No, there isn't. But you don't need to worry about me." He gave her a quick hug. "Go call the doctor."

An hour later Emma was carrying Jamie through the Braswell Hospital toward the pediatric unit, where Dr. Ted assured her they had a bed waiting. He wanted to put Jamie on intravenous antibiotics and to run some tests. In Emma's arms, Jamie felt too light, too small to be facing something so overwhelming.

Emma felt so alone. She suddenly wanted her granddad there with her. Then she started thinking about Daron McKay, and how he'd been watching over them for the past three years. Right now she wouldn't even complain about him being where he wasn't invited. Because never in her life had she felt so alone. And never had she wanted company more than she did at that moment.

As she approached the nurses' station, a somewhat familiar face stepped out from behind the desk. Samantha Martin, now Jenkins, smiled at the two of them. Duke's younger sister had a friendly openness about her. She'd married a couple of years ago, and from the tiny bump near her waistline, it appeared she might be expecting.

"Ted said you were on your way up." Samantha touched Jamie's brow and offered a reassuring smile. "And you've got quite a fever. Let's get you in bed and see if we can get you cooled down."

Emma followed Samantha down the hall and into a room with green walls and a view of an open field that lay beyond the hospital grounds. Samantha took over, placing Jamie in the bed, covering her with a light blanket and then kissing her forehead. Emma stood back, watching as the nurse moved about the room, turning the television on to a cartoon station and opening the curtains to give a clearer view of cattle grazing in the distance.

Emma stepped into the hall to take a deep breath. She could do this. They would survive. She closed her eyes to say a heartfelt prayer for her daughter.

When Daron pulled up to the office, Boone's truck was parked in front. Daron parked next to it and got out. Hard rain was falling from a sky heavy with clouds. He hurried through the front door, pulling off his jacket and tossing it on the back of a chair to dry.

"You look bad," Boone said, surveying him critically.

"Thanks. It's pouring."

"How'd last night's job go?" Boone poured him a cup of coffee. "Here. That ought to help."

"Or rot my insides." He sat down and put his booted feet on the top of the desk. "Not bad. The senator is a hard one to stay close to. Works the crowd like a…"

"Politician?" Boone offered.

"Yes, something like that." He tossed his cowboy hat on his desk and ran a hand through hair that tended to curl in this weather. Daron took a sip of coffee and grimaced. "Let Lucy make the coffee next time."

"You say the most hurtful things," Boone shot back, his mouth curving.

"Hurtful but honest." He took another sip of coffee and decided it wasn't worth it. "I'm going to Duke's for lunch. And coffee."

"Or maybe you're just hoping Emma is there. She's going to get tired of your version of babysitting. Or is this courting, Daron McKay–style?"

"I'm not babysitting or courting. Where did you get that? I'm…" He rubbed a hand across his cheek. Man, he needed to shave. "I'm just doing what I promised."

Boone held up a hand to cut him off. "Stop. Andy volunteered to go with us."

"I trusted Afiza."

"Yeah, you did. And we trusted her brother. That doesn't make you Emma Shaw's keeper. It isn't your fault Andy divorced her, or that he didn't list her as a beneficiary."

"You'd think his family would want to help out."

"But they don't," Boone said. They'd had this conversation a hundred times before. "You can't make sense of what doesn't make sense, my friend. So either you keep hounding her, trying to help when she doesn't want it. Or you walk away and let her live her life. The problem is, if you don't mind me saying so, that you kind of like being in her life. You're attached to Jamie. You like Art."

"They're pretty easy to like." He grabbed the mail piled on his desk and started opening envelopes. A few checks they'd been waiting for.

A letter from his mom. Why would she send a letter rather than call? He slid his knife under the flap of the envelope and pulled out a card. No, it was an invitation. He glanced over it.

"Something good?" Boone asked as he got up to pour himself another cup of coffee.

"My mom, making a point."

"What's that?"

Daron glanced at the photograph on the front of the invitation, of a smiling blonde and her too-handsome fiancé. He opened the card and read over the details. "My ex-fiancée is getting married. This is my mom's way of letting me know I've missed the boat."

"It isn't like there aren't plenty of boats out there." Boone lifted his cup of coffee in salute, and the light glinted off his wedding band.

"Spoken like a man who is tragically in love."

"Nothing tragic about it, my friend. So, will you go?"

Daron glanced over the invitation and then shot it into the wastepaper basket. "I don't have time for this. I'm going to run to the bank and make a deposit that will keep us solvent and help you pay off that pretty house you've built your wife."

He was heading for the door when the phone rang. He waited as Boone answered. Then he waited because the call seemed serious.

"Well?"

"First-responder call." Boone shot him a look that unsettled him.

"Who?"

"Art Lewis. He's cut his finger pretty badly and Emma isn't there."

"I'll drive on out there and make sure he's okay," Daron said as he headed out the door, Boone behind him.

"Might as well," Boone agreed. "I'll follow you in my truck."

As they left town, the fire truck and rescue unit were leaving the rural fire station that served the Martin's Crossing and Braswell area. Daron flipped on the first-responder light on his dash and fell in behind the emergency units.

It took less than ten minutes and he was pulling up to the small home where Emma lived with her grandfather. Art was on the porch, a towel wrapped around his hand. Daron jumped from his truck and hurried past the other first responders.

"What happened?" he asked as he reached the porch.

Art grimaced. "That tractor. I've been trying to get that nut loosened up for ages, and of course today it came loose and my hand slipped. I cut a hunk out of my thumb."

Art started to unwrap his hand and show Daron and Boone, who had joined him on the front porch.

Daron stopped him. "No, that's okay. Keep it wrapped. And you're pale, so why don't we take a seat and let the guys check you out?"

A first responder grinned as he stepped into the group and took over. "Art, you have a way of finding trouble. Wasn't it just last year that you set—"

Art cut him off. "Let's not go over the list of past sins or we'll be here all day."

The first responder took a look at the gash and shook his head. "You're bleeding pretty good here, Art. I think we need to get you to Braswell."

"Oh, don't look so worried. I'm not going to bleed out." Art started rewrapping the wound.

"We're going to dress this a little better," the first responder told him. "Let's get you to the ambulance and we'll be in Braswell before you know it."

Art planted his feet on the porch. "I only called you young roosters because I thought you'd bandage it up. I didn't expect you to haul me in."

"Well, Art, there are just some things we can't do in the field." The first responder held his own, but the corner of his mouth flirted with a smile.

"I'm not in a field. I'm on my cotton-picking front porch."

Daron laughed and earned himself a glare from the older man. "Art, I'll call Emma. She'll be glad you went to the hospital. Is she at Duke's?"

"No, she had to take Jamie in to the doctor. I figured she'd be home by now, but you never know what the wait time is going to be."

"Is Jamie still sick?" Daron asked as the first responder continued to look Art over. They had moved him to a chair.

Art glanced down at his injured hand and then back at Daron. He grimaced a bit as the first responder cleaned the wound. "Yeah, son, she's still sick. But she's strong and her mama has faith." Art turned his attention back to the first responder, who now seemed to be trying to help him to his feet. "Son, I said I'm not going. I can drive myself if I need stitches."

Boone walked up behind Art, his beat-up cowboy hat pulled low over his brow and a look on his face that told the first responders to take a step back. "Art, how about we drive you to Braswell to the ER? They can sew you up. Plus, you can check on Emma and Jamie while you're there."

Art pushed himself out of the chair. "Now, that's an idea. Thank you all for coming. I'll just take Boone's offer and let you all go on back to your jobs, or whatever you were doing before I got you called out here."

Daron shot Boone a look. "Really?"

Boone arched a brow and grinned. "We don't have anything else on the calendar for today, do we?"

"No, nothing else. And we both love to get Emma riled up. Let's go, Art." Daron led the older man down the steps and to his truck. "You aren't going to bleed all over my new truck, are you?"

Art stumbled a bit, but his voice, when he answered, was still strong. "I reckon if I do, you can get it cleaned up."

Daron laughed. "Yeah, I reckon."

The three of them crowded into the front of Daron's truck, Art in the middle. Boone leaned back in the seat like he was in his beat-up old recliner and happy as he could be.

"Now that it's just us," Art started, "why don't you tell me what you think Pete Shaw wanted the other night?"

Daron pulled onto the main road. "You knew that Pete was out there?"

"No, not at first. I heard Emma shout and then heard Pete mumble something about her trying to kill him. I was heading for my bedroom door when I heard you say something and I just figure you're a few years younger, so you might as well handle things."

"Thanks for the vote of confidence, Art. And I'm not sure what Pete's after."

"I guess I just figured you had some idea, since you're patrolling the place like an overworked guard dog."

"What's that supposed to mean?"

Art shot him a look. "It isn't like you can hide a pearly white Ford King Ranch like this. I'm old, I get up at night and I've seen you driving by like you're keeping an eye on the place. Emma has seen you. I guess she told you to mind your own business."

Daron kept driving. "I'm not patrolling. I'm just driving by on a public street."

"Call it what you want," Art said. "I call it patrolling. Emma calls it being a nuisance. I reckon you have your reasons."

"I'd like to be able to help out, Art."

"There's nothing you can help with, Daron. I know you mean well, but we've got it handled. We've struggled a bit, but things aren't so bad we can't deal with it. This hand might slow down patching up that roof, but we got a tarp on it yesterday and that'll hold us over until I can climb up there."

"But what about Pete?" Boone asked, entering the conversation with a quiet question. "What's he after?"

"He's an addict who believes there's more money than what he got. Emma has other concerns without Pete stirring up trouble for her. I told her to call his parents but she won't. She doesn't want anything to do with Andy's family."

"Don't you think they'd like to know Jamie?" Boone asked, his tone casual.

Art guffawed at that. "They know they have a granddaughter. But they're the kind that thinks they're better than others, and that Emma wasn't quite what they wanted for their son. They encouraged the divorce. I can't say I wasn't glad when the marriage ended, as Andy wasn't particularly nice to my granddaughter, but I'm sorry his family lost him."

"Art, what's wrong with Jamie?" Daron tried to ease back into the conversation, but he saw from the corner of his eye that it didn't work.

"Now, that's something you'll have to ask Emma. And I reckon if she wanted you to know, she'd tell you."

"She's been too busy telling him to leave her alone," Boone added.

Daron didn't thank his friend for his special brand of humor. He wanted answers, and this wasn't getting him anywhere. He drove faster, telling himself he wanted to get Art to the ER a little quicker.

It wasn't the truth. What he wanted was to get to Emma's side, sooner rather than later. He could tell himself it was because he was worried about Jamie, which he was. Or he could blame it on a need to keep Andy's widow safe.

He needed to keep a promise to a dying friend. When he'd made the promise to Andy, it was about a woman he didn't know and a baby not yet born.

Now he knew them. He knew Emma as a woman of strength and faith. She loved her little girl. She loved her grandfather.

Unconditional love.

Watching her, being around them, it made him want to be a better man. The kind of man she allowed into her life.

Chapter Four

Emma stood back as her daughter was examined by the on-call physician in the Braswell Community Hospital pediatric wing. The doctor smiled as he rubbed the stethoscope to warm it; then he winked at her daughter and told her she was brave and promised she'd be getting the best dessert once they were finished with the examination.

"She's a strong girl, Mom." The doctor listened, "Another breath, Jamie."

Jamie took a deep, shaky breath. She was still pale. Her lips weren't as pink as normal. It had been so frightening, that moment when Emma realized her daughter was gasping for air. She'd hit the call button, summoning a nurse as she tried to calm Jamie, telling her it was fine, to take slow, easy breaths.

A hand touched Emma's. Samantha Jenkins moved to her side. "I'm sorry—I was with another patient down in X-ray. She's okay, Emma."

Not a question, a statement of fact. Samantha's expression was reassuring as she gave Emma a quick hug.

Emma nodded, accepting the words of encouragement, but it didn't immediately undo her fear. Her hands trembled and she couldn't seem to stop the shaking.

"Let's step into the hall," Dr. Jacobs said, patting Jamie's arm. "I'm going to have a nurse come in and give Jamie her dessert options."

"Mommy." Jamie's voice was weak.

"I'll be right back, sweetie."

Tears filled Jamie's blue eyes. Emma leaned to kiss her forehead. She wiped away the tears that rolled down her daughter's flushed cheeks and she fought the tightness in her own throat.

"Your mom will be right back, kiddo. And I bet the two of you will share a brownie." Samantha eased in next to Emma. "I'll stay with you until she gets back."

Jamie nodded, her eyes closing as Samantha trailed fingers through her hair. Emma stepped into the hall where Dr. Jacobs waited. The elevators at the end of the hall opened.

Her grandfather stepped out and headed her way. Daron McKay followed. The fear that had cascaded over her gave way to relief. The tears she'd fought fell free and she sobbed.

"Let's take a walk." Dr. Jacobs inclined his head, directing her away from Jamie's room.

Her grandfather, his hand bandaged from the cut she'd been called about, and Daron, fell in next to her. She hadn't wanted to be alone. Now she wasn't. Tears continued to stream down her cheeks and she swiped at them with her hand until her grandfather handed her a clean, white handkerchief from his pocket.

Dr. Jacobs led them to a conference room with a table, bright fluorescent lights and molded plastic chairs. "It isn't comfortable, but there's more room if we're going to have several of us. Unless you'd prefer just the two of us having this conversation?"

"No, of course not." Her gaze skimmed past her granddad to Daron, standing in the doorway, his cowboy hat in his hands as he waited. "They can join us."

Dr. Jacobs motioned them all to the table. "Let's have a seat."

She sat down, the chair scraping on the tile floor. Daron sat at the end of the table, several chairs away. Her grandfather sat next to her.

He put his arm around her, giving her a light squeeze. The gesture was as familiar as her own reflection in the mirror. From the very beginning, that had been his way of comforting a lost and hurting girl. She was a woman now, and sometimes felt responsible for him, but he was still her strength.

Dr. Jacobs sat across from them. He was youngish, with dark hair and dark eyes, the smooth planes of his face covered in five o'clock shadow. Yes, he was older than her twenty-eight years. But he was still too young.

"Isn't Dr. Jackson in today?" she asked.

Dr. Jacobs smiled, because of course she'd made it obvious that she was worried. "Not today, but don't worry. I'm smarter than I look."

"I'm sorry," she started to apologize, and he stopped her.

"Don't be. I know I look young. I also know that your daughter is the most important person in your life and you want only the best for her. I'm the best. I wouldn't be here if Dr. Jackson didn't think that I was qualified for the position. So let's figure out what we need to do for your daughter."

"Okay." She met his steady gaze. "What do we do?"

He glanced over the file in his hands. "We

start with an echocardiogram. I'm worried about the ventricular septal defect, but I also think she has pneumonia. We'll do blood tests, start her on IV antibiotics and get her hydrated."

He listed it off, as if it were a shopping list. But it was her daughter. It was Jamie's heart. It was her life.

"She'll be okay," Emma heard herself say. Not a question. A statement of faith. God hadn't gotten them this far to let them down.

"She'll be great. I think she should stay in the hospital for a few days. And I also think we need to take a careful look at her heart because it might be time to repair the VSD."

"Open-heart surgery?" For years she'd dreaded those words.

"I hope not. We have options other than open heart. I'm an optimist." Dr. Jacobs gave her a steady look. "I'm also a man of faith. We'll do everything we can. And when we've done all we can, we stand on faith."

She nodded, closing her eyes against the fear, the hope, the onslaught of emotions that swept over her. A chair scraped. A hand settled on her shoulder. Without looking she knew that it was Daron. That he was there, standing behind her, the way he'd been doing since he got back from Afghanistan. It was guilt that kept him in her life. But today she didn't mind. Today his presence felt a lot like friendship and she wasn't going to turn that down.

Somehow she would get through this. Jamie would be okay. They would have the surgery, and she would be healthy. But it was good to have people to depend on.

"When will the surgery take place?" Daron asked, his voice deep, strong.

"I think sometime after Christmas. I want to know that she's strong enough before we send her down to Austin."

"Austin?" Emma asked, the reality of what he'd said hitting home.

Dr. Jacobs leaned a bit, making eye contact. "I'd love to tell you we could do the surgery here, but we can't. We'll contact specialists and she'll have the best of care."

"But you do believe we can wait until after Christmas?" Daron asked, his use of the pronoun *we* not lost on her.

"Yes, I think so. Unless there's a change, she isn't in any immediate danger. For now our main concern is this infection." Dr. Jacobs cleared his throat. "I know this is a lot to take in. What we want right now is for Jamie to rest, and for Mom to not worry."

"I think we can make sure that happens," Granddad said, patting Emma's hand.

"And we'll do our best, as well," Dr. Jacobs responded.

"Can I go back to her now?" Emma needed to see her daughter. She needed to hug her and to reassure herself that Jamie was okay.

"Yes. I ordered the blood test. We'll give her a little time to relax and then we'll take her down for the echocardiogram." Dr. Jacobs stood, the file in his capable hands. He handed her several printed copies. "If you have any questions, don't hesitate to ask."

"Thank you, Doctor." Emma looked down at the files in her hands, the words swimming as she blinked away tears. Ugh, she didn't want to cry. No more tears.

The doctor left, the door closing behind him.

Her grandfather steepled his hands on the table and cleared his throat. "I reckon you ought to tell Andy's parents about their granddaughter."

"I'm not going to call them. They don't want anything to do with her."

"They might want to know about this," her granddad pushed in his quiet way. "Em, she is their granddaughter."

"No, she isn't. She's *your* granddaughter.

There's more to grandparenting than a title and DNA. I'm not going to call them."

"Forgive—" her grandfather started.

"I will forgive," she conceded in a softer tone. "But I'm not through being angry."

She pushed back, the chair hitting Daron. She'd forgotten he was behind her. He grunted and rubbed his knee.

"I'm sorry," she said, her hand going to his arm. "I have to go. Jamie will wonder where I've gone to."

Boone Wilder was waiting outside Jamie's door. He tipped his hat, his smile somber. His presence made her falter, just a step. She'd gotten used to Daron's presence, his midnight drives past her house. Boone was more low-key with his interference.

"Boone," she said as she slipped past him. "You don't have to be here."

"Now, why wouldn't I be here, Emma?"

Arguing with him would have been pointless. It was their code. Whether as cowboys or soldiers, they stuck together. They took care of their own. She had become theirs when Andy died.

He followed her into the hospital room, where a nurse was setting up to draw blood. Samantha still sat next to the bed, Jamie's hand in hers. Her grandfather came in, not minding that the small room was crowded. He moved in close to his great-granddaughter and patted her hand. Jamie smiled up at him.

"Hey, Grand-girl, you sure do look pretty." He touched her nose.

Jamie managed a weak attempt at a smile and touched his bandaged hand. The gesture undid something inside Emma. She hadn't thought to ask him what happened. How exactly did he get hurt? How bad was the injury?

"You were working on the tractor, weren't you, Granddad?" she asked, watching as he moved his hand from Jamie's reach.

He winked at Jamie and then glanced up at her, his look a little more serious. "Just a little cut from that tractor."

"I told you…" She shook her head. Daron moved in behind her, his hands resting lightly on her shoulders. She breathed deep and relaxed. "I'm sorry I wasn't there."

And he was a grown man. He didn't want her telling him what he could or couldn't do.

"You don't always have to be there, kiddo. And I can get cut with or without your help. Boone and Daron came out and got me all fixed up. So right now let's worry about my ladybug."

Just like that, the room cleared. Boone and

Daron slipped into the hall. Samantha smiled down at Jamie, gave her a quick kiss on the cheek and told her she would check on that brownie. Then it was just the nurse drawing the blood, Jamie, Emma and her grandfather.

"We're going to put her on oxygen." The nurse said it quietly. "She's doing fine, but a little won't hurt. Also, we've got a line in and we're starting her on antibiotics and fluids."

"Thank you." Emma sank into the chair next to her daughter. "Do you feel better?"

Jamie nodded, her eyes scrunched, her cheeks pink from the fever. "I like brownies."

"Yes, you do." Emma swiped at a tear that rolled down her cheek. "I love you."

"I love you, Mommy."

Never had any words meant so much. Except maybe when her grandfather told her everything would be okay. She always believed him, trusted him.

Movement outside the door caught her attention. And then she heard the scrape of a chair on the tile floors. She glanced that way as Daron placed a chair next to the door and took a seat, a cup of coffee in his hand and his cowboy hat pulled low. He crossed his right ankle over his left knee and leaned back. It looked like he planned on being there for a while.

She should tell him to go home. But she couldn't. Not today, when it felt better knowing he was there. He'd managed to enter her circle of trusted people. She hoped he didn't let her down.

Daron woke with a start, rubbing his neck that had grown stiff from sleeping in the waiting room chair. He'd pulled it into the hall, next to Jamie Shaw's room. It was late. The halls were quiet, the lights dimmed for the night. The quiet whisper of nurses drifted down the hallways, but he couldn't make out their words. He glanced at his watch. It was a few minutes after midnight.

Standing, he stretched, rolling his shoulders and neck, and managed to feel almost human again. His back ached, but he could live with it. He'd been living with it for a few years. He took a careful, quiet step and peeked into Jamie's room.

Emma was asleep, like him, in a chair not made for comfort. Her head rested on the hospital bed. Her hand clasped her daughter's. Jamie was awake. She glanced his way, her eyes large in her pale face. He silently eased into the room and lifted the cup of water next to her bed. She shook her head and her smile wobbled. He hadn't been around too many kids in his life, but this one had his heart. She had from the moment he first saw her through the window of the nursery at this very hospital. She'd been pink, fighting mad and none too pretty.

He guessed she knew she had him wrapped around her finger. And that was okay by him.

Not wanting to wake Emma, he brushed a hand through Jamie's hair, then raised a finger to his lips. Her stuffed animal had fallen to the floor. He picked it up and tucked it in next to her. When she seemed content, he turned his attention to Emma. She had to be cold, curled up the way she was in the vinyl hospital chair. Looking around the room, he spotted a blanket folded on a shelf and returned to cover her with it. She didn't stir.

With a wave, he headed toward the door. Jamie watched him go, snuggling into her blanket and closing her eyes. He walked down the hall, not really sure where he was heading. Of course he wouldn't leave. He was used to pulling all-nighters. Sleep wasn't typically his friend, because in sleep the nightmares returned.

A soft light shone from a room at the end of the unit. He headed that way, curious. When he got there and peeked in, his curiosity evaporated. The chapel. The light came from a lamp illuminating a cross. On a shelf beneath it lay a Bible. A plaque hung on the wall next to the display, with the words "Thy word is a lamp unto my feet and a light unto my path. Psalm 119:105" engraved on it.

Out of habit, he took off his hat. After all, this was church. It was small. There were no pews. A minister didn't preach here on Sunday. But the room had a comforting feeling, as if Jesus might walk in at any moment, clasp a hand on a man's shoulder and tell him to let go of his burdens.

It was hard to let go of the burdens he'd been carrying for several years. He'd grown too accustomed to the weight.

When he thought about letting go, he wondered who he'd be without them. Without the burdens. He guessed it was wrong to think of Emma and Jamie as burdens; they weren't. They had actually become his anchor, keeping him grounded. Because without them, he might not have wanted to survive the last few years.

He might have given in to some other ways of easing the guilt. He had plenty of friends who had found comfort in the bottom of a bottle. He also had friends who relied on faith. They seemed better off, if he was being honest.

He focused on work, and on keeping Jamie and Emma safe. Fixing a fence from time to time when she'd let him, buying Christmas gifts that he had delivered to their house, so she wouldn't turn them away.

He eased into the seat by the window of the chapel. A picture hung on the wall with a verse about comfort. This room was meant to comfort.

He bowed his head, hat in his hands. He hadn't prayed in a long time. He guessed he'd never been much of a praying man. He hadn't been raised the way Boone had, going to church, having faith, believing it above all else. When he'd filled out the paperwork to join the army, he checked the Christian box because if anyone had asked, of course he believed in God.

He'd prayed for Andy to live. Now he would pray for Jamie. And God had better be listening. Because she was a little girl. She was three years old with her whole life ahead of her. She had a mom who would do anything for her. And she had a granddad who loved her "more than the stars in the sky."

That was what Art had told her when he said goodbye to Jamie, before Boone gave the older man a ride home.

Daron hadn't been raised going to Sunday

school. He'd been to church a few times with the Wilders. That was the sum total of his experience with prayer. But he felt as if he had the basics down. Petition God. Ask the Almighty to spare a little girl.

When he heard a noise, he looked up, heat flooding his face. He stood, nearly knocking the chair over in the process. He jammed his hat back on his head and faced the person standing just inside the doorway.

Emma, head tilted, dark hair framing her face, studied him as if she'd never seen him before. "I didn't expect to see you here." She brushed a hand over her face and shook her head. "Not that you wouldn't pray. That isn't what I meant."

He waited, a grin sneaking up on him, as she found words for what she meant. She was cute. He'd avoided that thought for a few years because Andy had been married to her and there were lines a man didn't cross. But tonight, in a softly lit chapel, sleep still in her eyes and her dark hair a bit of a mess, he couldn't deny it. He guessed his brain was a little sleep addled, too.

"I meant, I thought you'd come to your senses and left," Emma finished.

"Should I be insulted that you were surprised to find me in the chapel?" Daron teased. "Or because you thought I'd leave you here alone."

"Stop." She held up a hand. "Please, not right now."

She looked vulnerable and alone. Instead of arguing, he closed the distance between them and wrapped his arms around her, pulling her close. She didn't fight. That took him by surprise. He was more surprised when she rested her cheek against his chest.

"I'm glad you're still here," she whispered. "I'm so tired of being alone. I have Jamie. I have Art. And of course I have friends. But sometimes I feel so stinking alone."

"I'm not going anywhere, Emma."

She left his arms and walked through the room to the cross. Her head bowed. He watched from the doorway as she prayed. He marveled at how she kept going, even seemed to be happy most of the time. By the world's standards she didn't have much, but he figured she had more than most.

Eventually she turned around, her expression telling him she hadn't expected him to still be there, waiting for her.

"What happened between you and Andy's parents?" he asked as they walked back down the hall, past the nurses' station, past rooms where children slept, some alone and some with parents close by.

"Other than the money, you mean?"

Andy had mentioned the money to him, that he'd divorced her and made his brother, Pete, his beneficiary. Once Andy learned about the baby, he'd meant to switch it back. He hadn't. But there had to be more.

"Other than the money," he said. "Because Pete got the life insurance, correct?"

"Pete believes Andy had another policy. And I think he did, before we got married. But he dropped it because he thought what he got through the military was enough. Pete doesn't believe me." She shrugged slim shoulders and paused a few feet from Jamie's door. "They didn't believe Jamie was Andy's daughter. We divorced so quickly. He left for the Middle East soon after. It didn't add up to them. But I'm not going to beg them to see her, or invite them here to hurt her."

"But Jamie is their granddaughter."

"They told me if she's really Andy's, they'll take her away from me. It's an empty threat. They can't take her. But the fact that they'd threaten it is enough."

He took her by the arm and guided her in the direction of the waiting room, where he fixed them each a cup of coffee. She took a seat, propping her feet up on a coffee table. He handed her a cup and sat down next to her.

"Andy and I were friends but I don't know his parents very well," he said. "But if there is some way I can help…? Is that why Pete shows up every few weeks?"

"You really have to stop camping out on the road. We don't need for you to protect us," she told him as she lifted the cup to take a sip.

"I don't sleep a lot. Keeping an eye on things is the least I can do."

She set the cup down on the table next to her. "I don't know what to do about Pete. You losing sleep isn't going to change that. And it isn't helping you, is it?"

He ignored the last statement, because he wasn't going to get bogged down in the subject of nightmares and shrapnel injuries.

"Pete's on meth. He used to be a decent kid, but his brain is melting." The subject of Pete was easier to tackle.

"I agree. Andy knew it, too. I just don't understand why he…" She stopped and shook her head. "No use asking why. It won't change anything. I don't want you to feel as if we're your responsibility. We aren't. And we really are doing okay. Things are tight, but we've got this."

"I know you do."

But he couldn't walk away. If someone had asked him if it was the guilt that kept him tied to her, or something else, he would have avoided the question. He wouldn't even allow himself to think about all the reasons he stayed in her life.

He'd always prided himself on being loyal. A loyal man didn't let himself get involved with a friend's wife.

Even if that friend was gone and the woman in question was hard to walk away from.

Chapter Five

Jamie was released from the hospital on Saturday morning. Emma helped her put on the fuzzy slippers, the only shoes they had with them, and handed her the teddy bear Daron had brought her the previous day. Throughout Jamie's stay he'd remained close at hand. Emma had tried to tell him to go home, or to work, whatever he needed to do. But he'd refused. Instead he'd slept in a chair in the hall or the waiting room. He'd brought her coffee, insisted she eat, and he'd entertained Jamie with sock puppets he bought in the hospital gift shop.

A light knock on the door frame interrupted her musings. She turned, not surprised to see Daron standing there. Her heart did something crazy and unexpected. No, not unexpected. She was a living, breathing woman, so of course she noticed that he was tall with shoulders broad enough to lean on, arms that held a woman tight and a dimpled Texas cowboy smile that knew its own charm.

He'd been kind to them. He'd been there for her during some of her toughest days. She appreciated him. Even though he was a bit of a pain. Like a stray dog that just couldn't be convinced he needed to keep moving on down the road.

"Your chariot awaits," he said in a low voice as he removed his hat. "Art said to let you know he's got stew for dinner."

"You've seen Granddad?"

Jamie was tugging at her hand and whispering. Emma glanced down at her daughter and smiled.

"What do you want, sweetie?"

"Did Daron really bring a chariot?" Jamie whispered, her eyes round.

"No, honey, he didn't. That's just a saying. He brought his truck."

Daron stepped into the room, as if he'd been invited. Emma didn't know when, but in the past few days she had sort of invited him into her life. She certainly had leaned on him for the last few days.

But she didn't want to get used to it. She had Jamie. And Granddad. They were a family. Daron was only temporary. She'd been telling herself that for a few years now. Sooner or later he'd work through whatever it was that kept him up at night and he'd move on. Maybe he'd go back to Austin. Maybe he'd get married and have kids of his own.

Jamie was holding her arms up. To Daron. He gave Emma a quick look, asking permission. Her hesitation was brief; then she nodded. Daron lifted Jamie gently, her arms wrapping around his neck. Her grin split open and the dimple in her cheek deepened. It hit Emma that they could be father and daughter. Both had hair more blond than brown, unruly curls and that dimple. Hers in the left cheek and his in the right. It made them a matched set. Like bookends.

But they weren't father and daughter. She cleared her throat and took a deep breath, getting past the thick emotions that settled in her chest. Wordlessly she packed up the few things still scattered around the room.

"Ready to go home?" Samantha asked as she breezed into the room.

"All ready," Emma said. She held their overnight bag and the bouquet of flowers Duke Martin had sent from all the folks at Duke's No Bar and Grill.

"Here's the prescription." Samantha handed

her a paper. "We called it in to the Braswell Pharmacy. It should be ready. And Dr. Jacobs would like to see her in a week. He'll arrange for you to meet with the surgeon in Austin. Probably in the next couple of weeks."

Emma nodded, hoping her fear didn't show. Daron reached for the bag she carried. He hefted it over his shoulder and motioned her forward.

"Sam, thank you for everything." Emma hugged the other woman. "I'm glad you were here."

"Me, too. And if you need anything, just call."

Moments later they walked into bright sunlight and fresh December air, crisp and clear. The sky was the color of robin's eggs, the haze of heat gone. Emma drew in a deep breath, for brief seconds closing her eyes as she exhaled. When she opened her eyes, Daron still stood next to her, Jamie's head against his shoulder.

"You okay?" he asked.

"I'm good. It just feels good to be outside and to breathe fresh air." She motioned him forward and he continued across the parking lot in the direction of his truck, the pearl-white paint gleaming in the winter sunshine.

He'd installed a car seat in the back of the

truck cab. It didn't surprise her. Jamie gladly climbed in, tucking her stuffed animal under her chin and cuddling into the blanket Emma had brought for her.

"Time to go home," Emma said, kissing her daughter on the cheek.

When they pulled up to the house, Jamie perked up. Her dog was on the front porch, tail wagging. Granddad opened the front door as Daron pulled right up to the porch.

"We can walk, you know," she muttered.

"Of course you can," he said as he eased to a stop and pulled the truck's emergency brake. "But why do that when I can give you front-door service?"

She unfastened her seat belt but didn't move to get out. "Thank you, Daron. For everything."

He winked, a gesture telling her it didn't really matter. But it did. They both knew it. He'd seen how much it mattered. "Anytime."

What should she say to that? No, he shouldn't do this "anytime." Anytime required something more than his hovering on the periphery of their lives, rescuing them, protecting them. Out of some sense of obligation, she thought. And how long could he go on, feeling so guilty?

"Daron, it's too much," she said quietly,

stopping him from reaching in the backseat to unbuckle Jamie.

"Too much?"

She bit down on the corner of her lip, trying to explain, to find a way to release him from whatever it was that kept him tied to their lives.

"You don't have to do all this. I don't know what happened, but I know you feel some sense of obligation to us. You don't have to. I don't blame you for Andy's death." She studied his face, the shift of his eyes away from her, the way his throat moved when he swallowed. "Let go. It happened and you don't have to continue this, whatever it is."

"Friendship?" He smiled only faintly as he looked at her.

"Is that what it is? Or is it that you're still worried that you owe us something?"

"It isn't guilt, Emma."

She arched a brow.

"Okay, maybe some guilt," he admitted with an amused expression that didn't quite touch his eyes.

"You don't have to feel guilty. You didn't take anything from me. It was already taken. Andy left me. Our marriage had ended, because…" She shook her head. "No, I'm not going to discuss this right now. But we were over and I'm sorry if he said something that made you feel responsible for us. So stop. You don't have to watch over us this way."

"It's been a long three years, Emma. I consider you a friend. And I'm not one to walk out on a friendship."

"Friendship is a cup of coffee and a phone call, not midnight drives, patrolling my road."

He chuckled. "You make me sound a little creepy. But if it takes coffee and phone calls for you to consider me a friend, then I could use coffee. And we could all use more friends."

They sat there for several minutes as she tried to gather up the courage to truly let him in.

"I could use a friend," she admitted. "I've been so busy, I've lost track of the ones I used to have."

He held out a hand. "Then we start today as friends."

"And you stop the crazy stalker/protector thing you've been doing." She took his hand, his fingers strong around hers.

"Nah, I don't think I can do that." With that settled, he reached in the backseat for Jamie. Somehow he'd twisted things around and she'd accepted his interference in her life. All because he'd used the word *friend*.

She wanted to argue but couldn't. He had Jamie in the front seat with them, and he was buttoning up her jacket, as if he'd been doing it all her life.

Jamie's arms were around his neck. The perfect sunny day had disappeared as they'd driven, and the blue sky was now heavy with clouds. A few drops of rain splattered against the windshield.

Jamie leaned in, touching her nose against Daron's. Emma's heart stuttered over that moment, the gesture her daughter usually reserved only for mother-and-daughter moments.

Daron caught her eye and winked, but he couldn't know what it meant, to share that moment with her daughter. To him it was simply a cute gesture.

"We should go inside before this turns into a downpour," he suggested just as a deafening clap of thunder vibrated through the truck.

"We might be too late." Suddenly rain pounded against the dry earth and beat against the windshield of the truck. "Maybe it will let up soon."

"Yeah, I'm sure that's what Noah said after the first thirty days. Let's make a run for it. I've got Jamie. You get the bag."

They flew from the truck, heads down

against the drenching, but it did no good. They were soaked to the skin as they hurried up the steps and rushed through the front door. The house was warm, but a bucket sitting in the middle of the living room floor reminded Emma that the roof still leaked. Drat.

Granddad handed them towels. "I've got coffee brewing and lunch on the stove."

"Looks like we'd best take care of that leak first." Daron rubbed his hair and face with the towel and handed it back to him. "This rain isn't supposed to let up for a few days."

"Too wet to get up there and put down shingles," Granddad told him, leading the way through the living room to the kitchen. "The bucket will keep us from getting flooded out, and as soon as this clears up, I'll get up on the roof."

"Do you have another tarp?" Daron asked, taking the cup of coffee her grandfather poured for him.

Emma took Jamie from Daron's arms and pretended this conversation about her roof wasn't humiliating. She'd already patched it. And added the tarp the previous week in hopes that they could sell some cattle to pay for the new roof the old house so desperately needed.

"Yeah, I think there's one in the shed," Granddad answered.

Emma held her daughter close, draping a blanket around her. The two men went on discussing the roof.

She had to stop this. "We can fix the roof ourselves, Daron. You've really done enough. Our roof isn't your problem."

He stopped midsip, the cup poised in front of his mouth. His brows arched. "I hate to remind you, but I believe friendship was your idea."

Wide-eyed, Jamie was watching the adults from Emma's arms, her gaze shooting from Daron to Emma and then to her granddad.

"Why don't you put that little mite down?" her granddad suggested. "I bought her a new cartoon the other day."

"Thanks, Gramps, I will. Daron, please. You don't have to do this."

She walked away, leaving the two men staring after her. Their voices carried. She could hear their soft murmurs as she tucked Jamie in her bed, giving her the stuffed animal that was her favorite. It had been a birthday present from Daron.

In three years he hadn't missed a birthday or Christmas. There had been mysterious deposits in her bank account that he wouldn't take credit for. Groceries had been delivered.

Jamie snuggled up with the stuffed horse, holding it close to her face, brushing her cheek against the soft fur. She loved that horse. As Emma brushed a hand over her daughter's soft blond curls, Jamie's eyes grew heavy with sleep. Her little-girl lips turned in a slight smile that said her world was just as she wanted it.

After a few more minutes, Jamie slipped into sleep, her eyelids fluttering only once, her arms tightening around the pink horse. Emma tiptoed from the room. When she got to the living room, Granddad was tending one of his famous pots of stew, cooked on the top of the woodstove.

"Where is he?"

He turned, looking sheepish and guilty as he tugged on his whiskered chin and stirred the concoction in the cast-iron pot. "He left."

She peered into the pot of meat and vegetables, the broth thick and savory. She'd make rolls later to go with the stew. It was perfect for a blustery day in December.

"Gramps, why do you look so guilty?"

"I reckon *you're* going to tell *me* why." He reached for salt and added a dash. "We've been making this stew together for nearly twenty years, haven't we, kiddo?"

The memory took her back, the two of them finding ways to be a family. "Yes, we have. And you're avoiding the question."

He stopped stirring, and when he started to lick the spoon, she stopped him. He put the wood spoon on a plate and tugged at his beard again.

"I'm not getting any younger," he started. "I don't like to admit there are things I can't do. And things I wish you didn't have to do. There are days I'm more than a little angry with Andy for not getting the paperwork done to make you his beneficiary. I'm more than a little angry with his family for taking the money and not thinking about their granddaughter. But there isn't much I can do about that. We get by fine on my Social Security and what you make at the diner. And it won't be long before you have your degree. I guess if we had stayed in town years ago instead of buying this place, we'd be doing even better. It is what it is. But the one thing I can do for you is teach you to accept help."

"He's helped us enough."

"I don't think this is about what he thinks he owes you. It's about a man trying to be a friend. Or maybe a little more."

She'd been about to walk away, but the last statement stopped her. She looked up at her grandfather and shook her head. "You have clearly lost it. I'm the furthest thing from the type of woman Daron McKay would be interested in. He's here because he feels obligated. He thinks he owes us something because of what happened." And it still hurt. Andy had been her husband, her friend. He'd been everything she thought she wanted, and then he'd abused her trust.

He'd cheated on her.

He'd left her alone. As much as he had hurt her, she still missed him. She cried at night because he'd died too young.

Granddad put an arm around her shoulders and kissed the top of her head. "I might be talking like a grandfather who is proud of his girl, but I think you are everything any man worth his salt would be interested in. You're a strong woman of faith, a good mom and pretty as a speckled pup."

She nodded. "And you are still a little prejudiced when it comes to your only granddaughter. But this conversation is pointless." She stood on tiptoe and pulled him down to kiss his scraggly, unshaved cheek. "What are you and Daron up to?"

Then she heard the truck pull up out front,

saving her the trouble of interrogating her grandfather. She walked out the front door, leaving him to tend to his stew. She would tend to sending Daron on his way.

It was still raining when Daron left his place and headed back to Emma's. It had taken him less than fifteen minutes to find a tarp in the storage room of his barn. It would probably take longer to convince Emma to let him put it on her roof.

He pulled up to the old farmhouse. It was a decent place, just in need of some work. He jumped out of his truck and there she was, standing in the rain, the hood of her jacket covering her head and hanging down over her brow. She looked up at him with dark eyes and a mighty big frown.

"Go home, Daron. When it stops raining I'll fix the roof."

He took her by the arm and moved her toward the covered front porch with the lawn chairs and a small grill. She jerked her arm free and stomped up the stairs, as much as a hundred-pound woman could stomp. When she turned around to face him, he managed to keep a straight face.

She was the most kissable female he had ever met, with those rosy lips and that big frown, raindrops trickling down her cheek. He took a closer look to make sure they weren't tears. Nope. Just rain.

He'd been in Emma's life for a few years now. When had he started noticing her lips? Or the darkness of her eyes, like coffee on a cold winter day?

He grinned, just a little. Enough to earn himself another narrow-eyed glare. Back to business.

"I'm not going home. You have a sick little girl in there. The last thing she needs is a leaking roof. The last thing you need is for Andy's parents to use that roof and her stay in the hospital against you."

She paled at the mention of Andy's parents.

"Emma, I'm sorry. I shouldn't have said that."

She glanced away but not before he saw the moisture in her eyes. "I'll get to the roof."

"You're wearing yourself out. Let me do this." As they stood there, the rain slacked off a bit. "I checked the forecast. It's going to rain all week and this looks like the best time. I'm not going to stand here and argue with you."

"Of course you aren't. But if you're going up, so am I. You can't do this alone."

She walked off in the direction of the shed. He guessed she was going to get a ladder. He hurried to the truck and pulled out the supplies he'd brought from his place.

He was gathering everything up when Emma returned. Without the ladder.

"It's gone," she explained. "I know it was in the barn. I used it for the last tarp."

"Let's have a look. Maybe Art put it somewhere?"

She shook her head, but she walked past him into the house. When she returned, she didn't look too happy. "Art hasn't seen it."

"So someone stole the ladder?"

She shivered and pushed her hands deep into the pockets of her jacket. "Yes. It isn't the first thing that's been taken. Things have been disappearing for a year or so. Not much. Tools. An old saddle. Now the ladder."

"Pete?"

She shrugged. "Maybe."

"I'll head back to my place for a ladder. Emma, he has to be stopped. I'm worried that he isn't in his right mind."

"Because he isn't. I knew Pete before. He was a good guy. Always a little wild, but decent."

Daron opened the door. "Go inside, where it's warm. I'll be back in fifteen minutes."

This time she didn't argue. Instead she headed back inside and he went back to his place. It gave him time to think. Gave him time to clear his head.

When he got back she met him on the front porch, tiny in her big jacket with brown work gloves covering her hands. He wanted to talk her out of going onto the roof with him. He knew she wouldn't listen.

He moved his ladder into position and headed up to the roof with the tarp, tools and nails in the pockets of the tool belt buckled around his waist. She joined him up there. The rain had let up. It was easy to find the leak.

They stretched the tarp and pounded tacks to keep it in place.

He gave a quick look at Emma on the opposite end of the tarp, holding it as he tacked it to the aging, broken shingles.

"I'm going to need a pot of coffee after we're done," he called out against the wind.

She nodded but didn't answer. Her shoulders shuddered and she had to be freezing. He worked a little faster, getting the tarp down in record time.

"Let's go," he said. He motioned her toward the ladder. "You go first."

She went down as he held the ladder. The wind caught her jacket and she swayed a bit, but held tight. He waited until she was firmly on the ground and holding the ladder from there before he started down. Close to the bottom, the wind gusted. The ladder wobbled. He felt it going and jumped.

"Emma, get back," he yelled as he fell sideways, the ladder going in the other direction.

His body hit hers and he twisted to keep her from falling. Pain shot through his spine, making him see stars. The ladder clattered to the ground, and Emma's arms were around him.

"Are you okay?" she asked, her arms still surrounding him, her body close.

Daron took a deep breath and let his arms ease around her. Just for support, he told himself. But she felt good in his arms. She smelled good, like spring flowers and rain. He wanted to hold her a little closer, a little longer, but he knew better. "Yeah, I'm good. Every now and then I get hit with a spasm. Jumping off a ladder probably didn't help."

Still in the circle of his arms, he thought she leaned in close and sniffed. Soon after, she seemed to realize where she was and what she'd done. She pulled back abruptly. "Let's get you that coffee."

He started to reach for the ladder, but her hand on his arm stopped him.

"We're both soaked," she said. "Forget the ladder. Coffee and a bowl of stew are more important."

He followed her inside, where they both shed their coats and shoes. She moved immediately to the woodstove. He followed, holding his hands out to the warmth. The aroma of the stew filled the room. His mouth watered.

"Is that your stomach growling?" she asked, humor lacing her tone.

"Might have been yours," he answered.

Art called out from the kitchen that the coffee was ready. And he asked if they noticed that the roof wasn't leaking anymore. Emma laughed a little and the sound made him want to pull her back into his arms.

"Coffee sounds good," he said too quickly. But he needed to move away from her, away from temptation.

If he'd had any sense at all, he would have gone on home. Instead he stayed. For coffee. For a bowl of stew. For time spent with this family. Because they had entered his life as an obligation but in the past few years they'd become a little bit more.

He never really allowed himself to think about what that meant. To him, they were just more.

Chapter Six

❧

Sunday dawned cold and blustery but without rain. Emma bundled Jamie up for church while Granddad went out to warm up the truck. They were going to the Martin's Crossing Community Church for the potluck. After all, she'd promised Lily. It would be good to go to the small community church. Their own church in Braswell had grown over the past few years. Growth was good, but Emma had missed the smaller congregation that had once felt a lot like family.

Now she felt a bit lost in the crowd. She might have spent her first years in Houston, but she was a small-town girl at heart.

"Ready to go?" Granddad, dressed today in starched jeans and a button-up shirt, stepped into the living room. He carried the pie she'd baked.

"All ready," she responded. She reached for Jamie's gloved hand and the three of them walked out the door.

By the time they reached the church at the end of Martin's Crossing's Main Street, the sun had come out and was warming the air. Somehow it still smelled of winter, of snow, of Christmas. It helped that the nativity was up on the church lawn and the town was decorated.

Three weeks till Christmas. She sighed at the thought. She was nowhere near ready for the holidays. Worry assaulted her as she walked next to her grandfather, carrying her daughter in her arms.

Darker thoughts were dispelled as they entered the church and were greeted by Duke and Oregon, their daughter Lily at their side with one of the little ones they'd recently adopted. A little girl named Sally.

"Good to see you all this morning." Duke shook Granddad's hand and handed him a program. "You all can join the Martins. We're midway up on the left. There's plenty of room."

It was a good plan. To sit with Jake and Breezy Martin, Samantha and Remington, Brody and Grace. With the Martins they would feel as if they belonged in this congregation.

As they walked up the carpeted aisle, Jamie

spotted Daron. He was sitting with Boone Wilder and his large family, all of them taking up two pews. Jamie pulled away from Emma and headed for the man sitting at the end of a pew, his cowboy hat in his lap and a hand brushing nervously through his hair.

"Daron," Jamie said, immediately crawling into his lap.

"Hey, there's my favorite girl." Daron shifted her, then glanced back over his shoulder. "And her very serious mommy."

Jamie giggled.

Boone Wilder stood, holding out a hand to Emma and then to Art. "Good to have you all. Join us?"

Emma glanced longingly in the direction of the Martins. It would be easier, less complicated, to sit with the Martins. She could sit behind Samantha. She could sing and not be distracted.

But Art was already accepting the offer. There was a shifting of bodies to make room for a few more. It was no problem, Boone Wilder's younger brother, Jase, assured them. So somehow Emma landed in the pew next to Daron, her daughter sitting on both of their laps.

"You don't get to look more nervous than me," Daron whispered.

"What do you mean?" she responded.

"I don't go to church often. So I have the market cornered on nervousness. I can't believe sitting next to me is more nerve-racking than coming to church for the first time in, well, months."

"I think it might be."

He chuckled and leaned in, his head touching Jamie's. Emma's daughter laughed and snuggled against him. It was too much. It hurt deep down, where she'd placed her hopes and dreams for a future with a man who hadn't shared those dreams.

But she didn't want to think about Andy. Not today. She didn't want to think about how she'd lost him twice. Once when he cheated on her and then divorced her. Next when an IED detonated in Afghanistan.

She closed her eyes against the onslaught of pain.

Daron seemed to notice, because his attention refocused on her face and he shifted Jamie. His hand touched Emma's arm.

"I can't do this. It's too much." She held her arms out to Jamie to go.

"Don't leave on my account. I'll go."

"No. It isn't you. Stay and give Art a ride home, if you don't mind. I just can't breathe in here."

She took Jamie and left, knowing people were staring, whispering and wondering about her unusual departure. When she got to the truck she put Jamie in the seat, and then she climbed behind the wheel and waited until the world righted itself.

It didn't. Not for a long time. Her chest ached and it hurt to breathe. Jamie started to cry.

"So that's what a panic attack looks like," someone said from the open passenger-side door.

She jumped a little. "Oregon. I'm sorry. I shouldn't have run out like that."

"We do what we have to. But I didn't want to leave you out here alone. You're okay now?"

"I think so. Embarrassed but okay."

Duke Martin's wife, Oregon, climbed in with her. Jamie was happy, nibbling on a cookie and playing with a book. Oregon must have given those things to her without Emma even realizing.

"Don't be embarrassed. We all have stuff we work through, deal with. Sometimes it helps to talk to a friend."

Emma nodded, accepting the offer. They had become friends in the past year. "It was just leftover emotion. I have days when I think I'm over it, that I've moved past Andy's death, the divorce, the pain. And then it sneaks up on me."

"When you see your daughter sitting on the lap of a man who is decent and kind."

"He's in our lives because he feels guilty. He isn't her daddy, Oregon. Lately he feels like a friend. But we aren't his problem and I don't want to count on anyone else the way I counted on Andy."

"Oh, how well I understand. But will you do me a favor, Christian woman to Christian woman?" Her smile was amused and knowing.

"Okay, you know I can't say no to that."

"I do. Give God a chance. Let Him heal your heart and trust that there are good men out there, men who cherish and who are faithful. Men who won't let you down."

"I'll try to do that." She glanced at the clock on her phone. "You should go back inside. No need for us both to miss church."

"Why don't we both go back inside? The message was going to be short today and I'd say they're already moving on to the potluck. Or getting close to it."

Go back inside. She glanced over her shoulder at the pretty little church, the scene of her crisis. It wasn't as if she could avoid these people indefinitely, Daron included. "Okay."

They entered the church together, taking a seat on a back pew and listening as the sermon came to a close. From where she sat, Emma could see Daron. She watched the expressions on his face change, saw his pain, his guilt.

She could help him, she realized. He didn't have to feel guilty for what had happened. He should have healing. Maybe even find faith.

Years ago she'd learned that friendships happened for reasons a person didn't always understand. Some relationships were just for a season, to teach, and to help.

Maybe this friendship of theirs was meant to help him work through what had happened to him overseas. Maybe he needed her as much as she needed him.

There. She'd finally admitted it, at least to herself, that she did need him as a friend.

Ladies were washing dishes and men were wiping down tables and putting up chairs. Daron knew how to make himself useful. He took a load of chairs and headed for the storage closet, allowing a quick glance in the direction of the kitchen, where Emma helped do the dishes. The church fellowship hall had been overflowing until about thirty minutes ago, when the potluck meal wrapped up and people started gathering up their covered dishes, saying their goodbyes and heading home.

Daron could have left. Instead he'd remained behind, keeping an eye on the woman who had escaped him at the beginning of church.

"Are you going to keep walking or just stand there gawking?" Boone said, coming up behind him, pushing another load of chairs.

"I'm walking."

"You're just worried about her, right?" Boone winked as he said it.

"You know, some people think you're charming. I don't get it," Daron shot back.

"It's the dimples and the pretty eyes. I'm taken, though."

"I feel sorry for her," Daron shot back.

Boone laughed, loud and long enough to draw some attention to the two of them. Happiness could be so annoying. Daron pushed the chairs into the storage closet, and when he walked out, he flipped off the light and shut the door behind him, leaving Boone inside and in the dark.

Boone came out chasing after him, but Daron escaped to the kitchen, the women and Boone's wife, Kayla. The two of them slid

into the room, the women turning to stare.
Kayla gave Boone a sharp look and he managed a grin that had her eyes softening almost instantly. Daron tried that same look
on Emma, but she just shook her head and
turned back to drying dishes. Jamie sat on
the floor nearby playing with plastic bowls
and measuring cups.

"Art went on home," Daron told Emma as
he edged a little closer to her.

"I know. He said you'd give me a ride. You
really don't have to. I can get someone." She
glanced around at the dwindling crowd.

"I don't mind. Actually I thought you might
like to come out to the Rocking M. I haven't
been there much lately, but I think I might..."
He cut himself off. There were things he
didn't tell anyone. Not even the woman pretending to be a friend.

Boone knew. Boone, Lucy and Boone's
mother. Maria Wilder had a way of listening. It encouraged a guy to talk about his secrets and his fears.

"You might try what?" Emma asked.

"Putting up a Christmas tree. Making the
ranch a little more homey."

"I see."

"You could help. You and Jamie." He back-
tracked when she looked perplexed.

"I don't think that's a good idea."

People were moving around them. Older women in comfortable shoes, a mom with a toddler on her hip, one of the older men who seemed to enjoy being the only man in the kitchen. Emma started to pull away from him. And for whatever reason, he couldn't let her go.

"What isn't a good idea? Helping me put up a Christmas tree? Taking an afternoon to rest and have fun?" He saw the corners of her mouth tilt, just barely.

"Daron, stop trying to tempt me with that sweet smile." Her cheeks turned pink as the words slipped out.

"I have a sweet smile."

"You know you do. And you know that we can't do this. We agreed on being friends, but I can't do this, Daron."

"I'm confused. What is it you think I'm looking for?" He followed her across the kitchen, where she tossed the towel she'd been carrying into the pile of used towels and dishrags. "Oh, you think I want *more* than friendship."

She spun around to face him. "Stop. Just stop."

He put his hands up and took a step back. Behind him he heard Jamie. She toddled up, her blue eyes wide, watching the two of them. "I'm trying to be your friend."

"I know." Her features softened. "I guess I don't want to get lost in something that isn't real. I'm a mom. I'm divorced. In my heart I guess I'm a widow. My life is complicated right now."

"I'm sorry," he said, leaning in close to keep the conversation between them. "I pushed. And I probably teased. I just…want to spend the afternoon with you and Jamie. Something that doesn't include me driving past your place, pulling in and pretending I didn't mean to be there, or showing up at the diner just to check and see that you're okay."

"Are we friends or am I just your latest mission?" she asked, her eyes darting to see who might be close enough to hear.

"Friends."

"Then stop driving past the house. Stop checking on me."

"Help me put up my tree," he continued, watching as she weakened a bit and waiting as something that felt like hope flared up inside him.

"All right, we'll go. I have to let Granddad know we won't be home till later."

He gave her a sheepish grin that he hoped

would cover a multitude of his mistakes. "I already told him."

She stomped off, but he knew that it was more in protest than in irritation. He felt pretty pleased with himself. Then he melted a little because Jamie had stayed next to him. Her hand was on his knee and she looked up expectantly. He picked her up and her sticky hands touched his face.

"Well, kiddo, looks like we're going to put up a Christmas tree."

"Christmas presents." Jamie giggled and patted his cheeks again. She leaned close to his ear and whispered, "I want a puppy."

"I bet you do." He carried her to where her mom was gathering up her purse and jacket and Jamie's soft blanket.

"Come back anytime," Oregon Martin was telling her. "We know you have a church in Braswell, but you can consider us your second church family. And, Emma, we'll all be praying for Jamie."

Emma hugged the other woman tight. "Thank you."

Then she turned those dark eyes on him and he realized he was in over his head and he wasn't sure if he knew how to swim in these murky waters.

"Ready to go?"

She nodded. Oregon gave her a questioning glance, so he jumped in and said, "I told Art I'd give them a ride home."

Jamie chimed in. "And Christmas trees."

Oregon looked confused but she didn't ask.

They managed to escape with no further incidents. He draped the blanket over Jamie and placed a hand on Emma's back to guide her out the side door of the church and across the parking lot to his truck.

On the way to his place, she broke the silence, reaching to turn down the radio. "People are going to talk."

"Yeah, I guess." He didn't dare grin. "They probably already do. Mostly about how I've lost it and how I need to admit I like you. Mostly they say I need to cowboy up if I'm going to ask you out."

"They say those things?" she asked.

"And a few more."

"You aren't going to ask me out," she stated flatly, giving no room for argument.

He'd argue anyway. "If you say so."

"You're making this pretty complicated, aren't you?"

He laughed at that. "Yeah, I do like complications. But I'll be out of your hair for a few days. I have a security job in Austin and then one in Houston."

"Good," she said, but it didn't sound like she meant it. And he was glad.

"Don't worry—I'm not going to stay gone." Now for the serious stuff. "I'd really like to go with you when you go to Austin to the heart specialist."

She nodded but didn't say anything.

He guessed there ought to be a program for guys who couldn't stay out of dangerous relationships.

Step One, admit you like to be a hero…

Chapter Seven

Emma had driven past the Rocking M. By most standards it was a smaller ranch, only a few hundred acres. It was still quite a bit larger than her grandfather's small farm. The front of the property was surrounded by white vinyl fencing. The driveway was blacktop, not gravel. The house at the end of the blacktop was a fantastic stucco, wood and stone lodge home with a covered front porch, stone-lined flower gardens and a few willow trees. In the distance she spotted the stable and other outbuildings.

"I shouldn't let it sit empty," Daron said as he pulled into the garage.

"Then why do you? Your parents used to stay here quite a bit."

"They got tired of the drive and they aren't really ranchers. My grandfather, my mom's dad, had a ranch. She thought she wanted that life back, then realized she wasn't much of a country girl anymore."

"So they handed it over to you?"

"Yeah, they did. Boone would tell you I'm not much of a rancher, either. But I'm not ready to give it up."

They entered the house through a utility room and then walked down the hall to the kitchen and great room with vaulted ceilings and large windows overlooking the country-side. Emma put Jamie down, but her daughter was unsure of this big new space, the hard-wood floors and shiny kitchen. Jamie held tight to her hand, eyes wide, studying the sur-roundings.

"I don't have any toys," Daron said, his ex-pression troubled.

"No one would expect you to."

"I do have coffee, however," he offered. "And a tree."

He pointed to the giant tree devoid of dec-orations. It was situated in front of the large windows in the living area.

"You planned this?"

"Not really. I wanted a tree. Today, when you showed up at church, I thought you'd probably enjoy decorating it. Or Jamie would."

"Then we should have that coffee. Where are the decorations?"

"The decorations are in the garage," he said. "I'll get them and you start the coffee. There might be instant hot chocolate in the pantry, if Jamie would like that. And cookies." He'd obviously thought of everything.

"I'll take care of it. You get the decorations." She watched him walk away; then she circled the kitchen with its dark cabinets, granite countertops and appliances that made her want to cook. And she didn't really like to cook.

She found the coffee and started a pot brewing. Jamie sat on the floor nibbling a cookie that Emma gave her. She leaned against the counter and watched her daughter jabber to herself. Jamie looked up at her, all wide-eyed and sweet. She looked so much like Andy. Sometimes it was so hard, seeing his face, his expressions, on their little girl.

Even though she didn't want to get lost in the past, there were days she wondered if he would have come home to them, been faithful, been a husband and father. After all, they had Jamie together. Would they have gone through with the divorce had they known Emma was pregnant?

They were all questions that would never

be answered because she and Andy had never gotten the chance to talk, except for that one phone call when she'd told him she was pregnant. He'd deserved to know.

"Everything okay?"

The question startled her. She regrouped and nodded. "Yes, just thinking."

"I see it, too. How much Jamie looks like him."

"Yes, and someday she'll want to know." She left the sentence unfinished. But they both knew. Someday Jamie would want to know about her dad.

"I'm sure she will. I'm sorry." He set the tubs on the floor and stood there, tall, strong, a little bit lost. She liked that about him, that little bit of vulnerability in a man who always seemed strong.

She picked up the coffee cups she'd found and poured them each a cup. She held one out to him. "Here's to friendship and forgetting the past. To letting go."

"A nice lecture hidden in a phrase of good cheer." He took the cup and lifted it in a salute.

"It wasn't," she started. "Okay, a little. Honestly we all have things we have to learn to let go of."

"If it was as easy to do as it is to say."

His expression shuttered and he walked away, taking the cup of coffee with him and stopping by the tree. Emma picked up Jamie and followed.

She didn't ask questions, not at the moment. Instead she sat in a rocking chair near one of the floor-to-ceiling windows and watched as he opened boxes, occasionally stopping to take a drink of his coffee.

Jamie climbed down off her lap and walked toward the box of glittery red ornaments. Daron handed her one and helped her hang it on a low branch of the tree. Emma moved from the rocking chair and lifted a laminated card with a ribbon attached. The angel and manger scene on the front didn't set it apart from any other Christmas card. She turned it and read the inscription on the back.

"Dear Soldier. Thank you for serving our country and keeping us safe. Jesse. Third Grade."

The words undid something inside her, something tightly wound that she usually kept a hold on, to keep her emotions safe, unattached from this man who had been watching over her for three years. That something unraveled a bit and she swallowed quick to keep it from turning into tears that were burning at the backs of her eyes, tightening her throat.

She reached for another ornament, an angel colored in childish scribbles. Also laminated and a ribbon attached.

"Don't cry," he warned in a low voice.

"I'm not going to cry."

He pushed a tissue into her hand. "Yeah, you're going to cry. You're starting to get emotional, thinking I'm sentimental. I'm not. It just seemed a waste to throw away an art project some kid put all that work into."

"Of course," she said, shoving the tissue into her pocket. Unused.

"There are letters, too. Don't start reading them or we'll be here all night."

She shook her head. And as he helped Jamie hang another bright red decoration, she hung a card with a picture of the baby Jesus and on the back, a note from a little girl named Annie whose daddy was serving in Iraq and so she prayed for all the soldiers.

There were more. Letters. Cards. Homemade ornaments. From elementary school children across the country who had signed with first names, the words misspelled and sometimes smudged. But they told a story of a soldier who had cherished each and every missive.

No, he wasn't sentimental. And as she read through the cards he found crayons and plain paper for Jamie to add her own work of art to his tree. Her heart tugged a little because she really did want this man for a friend. If friendship was easy and didn't include strings.

"I asked him to go," he said while bending over Jamie, without looking at Emma. "That day, when the boy came to get us, to help his sister. I asked Andy to go with us. I didn't think it would be a big deal."

"Of course you didn't," she answered, looking up to meet his gray eyes. He quickly looked away.

He gave Jamie a few more crayons and told her he liked the tree she was coloring. She told him with a smile that it was Baby Jesus. He agreed that it was a very good Baby Jesus.

"I knew about you, and about the pregnancy. I wouldn't have put him in danger."

"I know you wouldn't. He made the decision to go with you. It wasn't your fault. It wasn't his fault. We can't live our lives second-guessing ourselves."

"Of course." He straightened, stretched and pasted on a look that was probably meant to appease her, to stop her from pushing the conversation further.

A friend would ask if he was okay. A real friend. She wasn't sure if she qualified yet.

But here she was, helping him decorate his Christmas tree. She'd made coffee in his kitchen. She should push, get him to talk.

She let her attention drift to her sleepy little girl. Emma reached and Jamie went straight to her, arms out. She carried her to the sofa and snuggled her under an afghan before returning to the tree and to Daron. He had gone back to decorating.

"It wasn't your fault, Daron," she repeated as she stood next to him to hang a decoration. "Life isn't fair. It wasn't fair that my parents died in a freak car accident on wet roads. It wasn't fair that Andy died. Or that his parents refuse to believe Jamie is their granddaughter. It isn't fair that Pete is addicted to meth. Life isn't fair. But it's beautiful and complex. Every day I watch my daughter learn a new word, smile at something she's only just discovered. It's beautiful."

"It is beautiful." He looked down at her, and his gaze softened. "You…"

Emma held her breath. Because there weren't supposed to be moments like this. She was a single mom. He felt attached to them because of an event that had been out of his control. But the thread between them became a tangible thing. The air in the room buzzed as the moment stretched out. His fingers barely connected with her cheek but somehow pulled her up on her tiptoes, as if that invisible string was lifting her to meet him.

His lips touched hers. He tasted of coffee and cookies. It was warm and inviting and it made her feel truly alive to be in his arms. She hadn't felt alive, not like this, in a very long time. She'd simply been existing, being a single mom, a college student, a waitress.

For those few minutes in his arms, she was more. As his lips grazed her cheek and hovered near her temple, she wanted to be more than the solitary person she'd become. She wanted to trust her heart. Because this man was good and kind. He cared deeply.

He kept cards from schoolchildren he'd never met.

But trust was such a fragile thing and hers had been broken, shattered by Andy's infidelity, his willingness to walk away when he realized she didn't fit in his world or his plans for the future.

The heart was a funny thing. Once broken, it tried to avoid being broken again.

She slipped from his arms, the invisible string untethering so that she could back away. She touched her lips, still feeling the aftereffects of the kiss.

"I'm sorry," he said calmly. Hadn't he felt what she felt? Maybe that was the part of her heart she shouldn't trust, the part that felt so much when others seemed to feel nothing in return.

"Don't." Her hand slid from his shoulder. "It was a kiss, nothing more."

"Sure, nothing more," he said, the words sounding unsure. Maybe he wasn't as strong as she gave him credit for.

It was time to change the subject, to let the moment go.

"The tree looks beautiful. And I do love the homemade ornaments. Do you use them every year?"

He glanced at the tree, as if he'd forgotten its existence. She hid her amusement, then chastised herself for being so pleased that he seemed a little off-kilter.

"We're going to discuss the tree right now?" he asked, brushing a hand across his mouth.

"It seemed safe."

"Okay. Yes, I do. I put the tree up and water it and then I go to the Wilders'."

"Why?"

He let out a sigh. "This is the problem with women. Kiss them and they want to know all your secrets."

She heard the humor in his tone and a little bit of frustration. She decided to go with humor. "Kiss and tell, McKay."

"I don't sleep at night. Thus my stalkerish behavior, driving past your house, making sure you're all safe and sound. I pace a lot."

"Nightmares?"

He put the lid back on one of the tubs that had held decorations. "Yeah. Nightmares."

"You were injured, too."

He nodded at the observation. "Yes. I was hit with shrapnel."

"We've never discussed this." She picked up a card that had been left on the coffee table.

"We weren't friends," he said with a grin.

"No. And now we are. So tell me about the injuries."

"Oh, you're one of *those* friends. The type that believes she has a right to know everything."

"Something like that. After all, you know everything about my life."

He picked up their coffee cups and headed to the kitchen. Her phone rang as he was pouring more coffee.

Daron listened to Emma's phone conversation. Even hearing only one side, he knew there was a problem. And it sounded serious, meaning she'd have to head home. He poured out the coffee and hit the power button on the coffeemaker. She ended the call.

"The tiller is gone. I don't know why Granddad was out in the shed, but he said it's practically empty. We don't go out there much in the winter." She slipped the phone into her pocket. "I can't afford this. I know it's Pete, although I don't know why he targets my family. I don't want to press charges. But I can't support his drug habit."

"He's going to have to get help. And if that means you pressing charges, then you have to do that. Let's head on back to your place. Did Art call the police?"

"Yeah, the nonemergency number for the county. They'll be out tomorrow to take a statement and a list of missing items."

He watched as she woke Jamie, holding her daughter close and trying to maneuver her arms into her jacket.

"Take the blanket. Then you won't have to stuff her into the jacket."

She nodded and wrapped the blanket tightly around Jamie. "Thank you. I'll get it back to you tomorrow."

"I'll be gone on a job."

Her eyes darted his direction. "Oh, that's right. I forgot."

The strangest thing happened; he realized he'd miss her. He guessed it wasn't the first time he'd had that thought. How did you miss a person when she wasn't a real part of your life? He guessed that after today, he'd miss her more.

He could call that kiss a mistake. Or just a moment. But what it did was change things. It changed a lot when a man kissed a woman, and when she stepped away, his first thought was how to get her back. And keep her.

The job would give him time to get away and put things in perspective.

"We should go. Before your granddad starts a search on his own." He laughed it off, but he wasn't sure it was really a joke.

"He did mention tire tracks at the side of the road. He said it looks like they went north."

"Maybe I should hire him?" He took Jamie from her. The little girl wrapped her arms around his neck.

"Only if you switch your business from security to private investigator."

He shifted Jamie to his left hip and pulled the keys out of his pocket. He winced as a spasm tightened in his lower back. Emma caught the look.

"I'm fine," he said.

"Of course you are. I didn't say anything."

When they got back to her place, he parked next to Art's old truck. Jamie was still sleeping. He got her out of the backseat. As they headed for the house, Art stepped out on the front porch.

"I wasn't expecting the two of you to head back here. I can hold down the fort." Art showed them his .22.

"Art, you have to put that away." Emma stepped up on the porch and took the weapon from her granddad. "That isn't going to solve anything."

"If it's Pete, he's hopped up on meth. You don't know what he might try next."

"He won't hurt us," she insisted.

Daron wanted to argue Art's side. Pete might hurt them. Instead he handed Jamie over to Emma and took the gun from her. "We'll put this away. And, Art, let's have a quick look in the shed. But we aren't going to touch anything. Let's make a list of everything you thought was in the shed and things you think might be missing. If you have paperwork on the tiller, that would be helpful."

"I have it filed," Emma said as she walked through the door Art had opened for her.

Daron followed Art to the shed at the back of the yard. "Art, I'm going to be out of town a few days."

"I'll keep them safe for you."

Daron opened the door to the shed. Did he argue that it wasn't for him? That they weren't his to keep safe? They were Art's family. But he didn't argue. Emma needed to focus on Jamie, on the upcoming surgery. She didn't need to worry about Pete and what he might do next.

Sometimes a man made a decision that would change everything. He guessed he'd been making decisions like that since he got back. Including the one he was about to make.

"If something happens, call me. And I'll make sure that either Boone or Lucy drives by here, just to check on things."

Art peered into the inside of the shed. "That's a lot more than a guilty conscience talking."

"I'd kind of like to think it's a thing friends would do for friends."

Art stepped out of the shed and he looked Daron head-on. He might be getting older, but Art Lewis was still a tough old man and the look on his face wiped away any humor Daron felt.

"Sure, okay. But let me give you some advice, Daron. Back in my day, if a man liked a woman, he just came out and said something. Usually he started out with 'I sure like that perfume.' And then he might ask if she'd like to catch a movie or get some ice cream."

"Ice cream, Art?" Daron couldn't help laughing.

Art gave him a sheepish look, his blue eyes twinkling.

"Well, I guess young people these days don't get ice cream."

"Maybe if they're fifteen."

"You're wearing my granddaughter's lipstick on your cheek. I guess ice cream would be a mite silly at this point."

Daron wiped at his face while pretending serious interest in the contents of the shed. "What was hanging on the hooks?"

"Some halters and a couple of bridles. Emma won't be happy about that. One was her show bridle. Not that she's had much chance to show. She had to sell her good mare. Shame, really. She's quite the trainer."

"When did she sell the mare?" Daron didn't

know why it mattered. He didn't want to think about why he was asking.

"Six months ago. She decided college and a way to support Jamie were more important than raising horses." Art said it over his shoulder as he looked around the shed.

"Who bought her?"

"Duke Martin. Probably hoping she'd be able to buy the horse back someday."

"We'll find her stuff, Art."

"Don't break her heart in the process. Andy did a number on her. She's not gone out with anyone since he left her. She says Jamie is her life and she doesn't have the time or energy for a relationship. But she's young. Too young to give up."

"I don't think she's giving up," Daron said. He closed the door of the shed. "The tiller, bridles and halters. You'll have to tell Emma because the police will need descriptions."

"Yeah, I know. I just hate it. It's like Andy took a big chunk out of her heart and his family has been chipping away at the rest ever since."

"We won't let them," Daron assured the older man. "We'll keep her safe."

"I'm guessing you are part of the 'we'?"

Daron didn't know how to respond to that.

He didn't feel like the person Emma should count on. Not when he was the person who had put her in this situation in the first place. One moment. One decision. Lives changed forever.

Because of his decision to ask Andy to help them out, Daron was now in Emma's life. In Jamie's life. In Art's life. When he'd started on this journey he thought it would be a short one. He'd get home, make sure they were okay and taken care of. But here he was, three years later, and he was still in their lives.

No escape route. He guessed he'd planned the mission without a clear way out.

Chapter Eight

The weather had warmed by Friday. Emma left the grocery store and headed for her truck, a bag under each arm. She'd worked the breakfast shift at Duke's, and as soon as she picked up Jamie from Breezy Martin's house, she was heading home to fix soup for Art. He'd caught a cold and wasn't doing well.

It didn't help that the house was drafty and damp. She'd build a big fire tonight and they'd have something warm to eat. She stored her worry for a later day. She didn't have time for it right now.

She definitely didn't have time to get sick. She could feel the virus tickling her throat and lurking in her head. She refused to give in to it. She didn't have time for that, either.

As she got in her truck, she waved at Boone Wilder. He was getting out of his truck and heading into Duke's. If she had more time she'd talk to him, tell him he didn't have to take over where his friend left off. She didn't need their bodyguard services. If Boone wanted to help, he should convince his friend Daron to move on with his life.

Three years was too long for one man to be stuck in the past. Stuck worrying about her. Stuck in his own nightmares. And because she knew that about him, she now worried about him.

She liked him.

Purely as a friend, of course.

It was easy to let him be a friend. No strings attached. No complications. No worries that she wouldn't meet his parents' standards. No fear that she wouldn't fit into his world. No heartache when he realized he'd married a woman who would never feel comfortable in his world.

He would never hurt her because she wouldn't give him the chance.

She started her truck and backed out of the parking space, waving to Oregon Martin when she appeared at the front door of her shop. Oregon's All Things was just that, a shop with a bit of everything. All handmade by Oregon.

The truck shuddered a bit as she shifted

gears. Like everything else on the farm, the truck needed repairs. Actually, if she was completely honest with herself, it needed to be replaced. She started it every day with a prayer that it would keep running. One more day. Her prayer for so many things.

She cranked the radio up. If she listened to music, if she sang along, it distracted her. It also meant she couldn't hear the death knock in the engine, telling her it wouldn't last much longer. Her worrying wasn't going to change things, so she might as well be happy where she was in life.

Where she was wasn't so bad. She rolled down the windows because it was damp and chilly but it felt good. The air smelled clean, like farmland and winter. The song playing on the radio was a favorite of hers.

She was going home to fix soup and the yeast rolls she'd put in the fridge the previous evening. She had a half dozen steers she planned to take to the auction. The money would get them through the next few months. It would help while she was in Austin for Jamie's surgery.

The surgery. Thinking of it caused a tight knot to develop in her stomach. Sing, she reminded herself. About peace. "It Is Well" came on the radio. One of her favorite versions of the song. A song about a man who continued to think it was well with his soul, even after the loss of family and fortune.

"Whatever my lot, thou has taught me to sing. It is well…"

Suddenly the engine popped and sizzled, and the truck rolled to a stop.

She leaned her forehead against the steering wheel and laughed. Crying would have taken too much energy and she doubted it would get her home. Besides, it was just another stupid thing to get her down, to steal her joy, to rob her of peace.

No, she wasn't going to let it get to her. She leaned back and thought about her tired feet and the two-mile walk back to town because her phone was dead. She gathered up her purse, her tips for the day stashed safely inside, buttoned her jacket and stepped out of the truck. Back to town was definitely closer than Jake Martin's house, where Breezy had Jamie.

The wind whipped at her hair. She pulled up the hood of her jacket and started walking. She didn't make it fifty feet when a truck eased in behind her. She turned as the gray Dodge moved to the shoulder. And then she started back toward her truck, picking up the pace when she heard the door of the other truck creaking open and slamming shut.

"Emma. Wait."

She didn't wait. Instead she ran to her truck and climbed in, locking the doors. She watched in her rearview mirror as Pete hurried to her truck. He was thinner than the last time she'd seen him. His light-colored hair was thin and greasy. There were sores on his face.

"Emma, I just want to talk."

"I don't want to talk. Pete, just go. I don't have anything. If I had money would I be driving this truck?"

He braced his hands on the top and peered in at her. His eyes were watery and rimmed with dark shadows. She felt for him. He hadn't always been this person. But he'd made the wrong choices.

"I need help. I need money." He closed his eyes but continued to rest against her truck. "I'm tired, Emma. I can't keep doing this."

"Then get help. Go to your parents and tell them you need help."

"I haven't seen them in months. I can't see them because I don't want them to know. You have to help me." He looked up at the overcast sky. "I need five thousand dollars."

"Oh, come on, Pete, even I know that meth isn't that expensive."

"I owe some people. Some really bad people."

"I'm sure you do."

"No, you have no idea." He shook his head. "I'm warning you. I'm in with some bad people. I've been dealing and I owe them."

"Did you take their money, Pete? Or use up the merchandise?"

"I don't have time for this, Emma. I just need money. If you could loan me some money. You were Andy's wife. I'm your brother."

"Andy divorced me."

"I know. I'm sorry." He looked about to cry.

She rolled down the window, unafraid. "Pete. You're strung out and you need to sleep. Get some help. Go to your parents. It isn't as if they don't know."

"I can't." He breathed in, his lungs raspy, his hands on the truck shaking. "I can't. But you have to understand. These people are bad."

"What are you saying, Pete?"

"These aren't the type of people who forgive."

"Okay, fine. They don't forgive. You should

go. You're starting to scare me and I need to get home to my family."

"How's Jamie?"

"None of your business."

He brushed a hand over his face. "Let me help you with your truck. I should help you. Andy would want me to do that."

"Pete, you don't have to help me."

This guy, who had been stealing from her a week ago, now wanted to help?

"Yeah, I can help. Let me look at the engine. Or I can call for a wrecker."

"You could do that for me. But then you have to leave. And, Pete, you have to get help."

"I wish that was possible." He pulled his phone out of his pocket, then shoved it back in. "Never mind. Your watchdog is here. I'll leave."

He took off at a run back to his truck. She watched in the rearview mirror and then she got out of her truck as Boone Wilder approached, looking menacing with his hat pulled low and a glower directed at the other man, now in his own vehicle.

"What did he want? Did he stop you here?" Boone was reaching for his phone.

She put a hand on his to stop him. "My truck engine blew. He actually stopped to help. And I don't know, maybe to warn me. Or ask for money. I'm not sure."

"What did he say?"

"He's in with some bad people and he owes them money. I'm not sure why that would worry me, but he acted as if it should."

Boone continued to watch as Pete turned on his vehicle and left. "Yeah, it should worry you. If he's in with the wrong people, it should worry us all. I don't get how someone gets into that stuff. But they do. Good families, dysfunctional families, it can happen to anyone."

"Yes, it can. I told him he needed to get help."

"He isn't interested?"

"Not at this point." She pushed the truck door open. "My phone is dead. I'm supposed to pick up Jamie from Breezy's. And now this."

He wrapped her in a friendly hug. "I'll call a wrecker and we'll go get Jamie."

"Thank you," she said. "It's been a long day."

"A long year. Or three?"

"Yeah."

Boone pulled out his phone, made a couple of calls as he paced the shoulder. "The wrecker will drag the truck out to your place.

Unless you have somewhere else you want it taken?"

"No, have him take it to my place. It isn't going to get fixed for a while."

She wasn't going to say how worried she was. She needed this truck. It was her only transportation to work. But she still had the steers. She could use that money to get this truck fixed or get a decent older truck. They would get by.

"I can loan you one of our farm trucks," Boone offered as he opened the passenger door of his truck for her.

"We'll be fine."

"I know you will, but I'm offering."

She nodded and blinked back the moisture that welled in her eyes. She wouldn't cry.

And she wasn't going to allow herself to wish that Daron McKay was in town. She'd never felt this before, this need for someone, to lean on them. She had her granddad. She had Jamie.

So why did she feel so lonely? Why did she want to call Daron and tell him about her rotten day?

The screen door of the camper banged shut. Daron rolled on the couch and covered his face with the blanket. Or tried to. The blanket wouldn't budge. He yanked on it and tried to move, but a heavy weight held him pinned.

"Get, you smelly mutt." He didn't remember letting the dog in, but he'd been so tired when he got home that morning he hadn't really paid much attention.

The dog groaned, and then something hit his foot. Hard. Daron sat up, pushing the dog to the floor in the process. He reached fast for his sidearm and then he flopped back on the miniature couch.

"Go. Away," he snarled at Boone as he dragged the blanket back over his face. "I drove straight home from Houston after the event was over last night."

"Why didn't you stay in Houston and rest up?" Boone took his customary place in the recliner and kicked back, hat low and arms crossed over his chest. It looked like a casual pose. Daron knew him well enough to know it was anything but.

"I wanted to get home." He didn't want to go into reasons. He didn't want to talk about missing Emma Shaw. Just thinking about it made him feel like the worst kind of man.

"Okay, well, did your rush to get home have anything to do with Emma?" Boone asked.

"What? Emma? No." Daron paused for a

moment. Then he went on. "Is she okay? Is Jamie okay?"

"Yeah, she's fine. I just gave them a ride home."

"A ride home?" Daron reached for his boots and pulled them on. He pushed the dog away. The collie had a thing for lying on his shoes.

"From what I could tell, her truck engine blew out. She's fine. No transportation now, but she's okay. She's about the toughest woman I know. When I left her, she was heading to the field to hay their cattle. Art's down with a cold."

"You didn't offer to help?" He was already pulling on his jacket. Out of the corner of his eye, he saw Boone grin. He got a little suspicious. "What?"

"Nothing." Boone raised his hands. "I offered her a truck. She said no. I offered to help her feed her livestock. She said she does it every day."

"I have a farm truck at the ranch. I'll take her to get it." Daron had a hand on the door, but he remembered his manners. "Thanks for letting me know, Boone."

"Anytime. One more thing." Boone pushed himself up from the recliner and followed him out the door. "Pete was there when I found her on the side of the road."

"Maybe you should have started this story with that, rather than finishing it?"

"I'm telling you now, so relax. She said he kept mentioning he's in trouble with some bad people."

"Great. Leave it to Pete to get in with some drug cartel. He needs to go to rehab."

"He needs money. Sounds like he owes someone a lot of money, and it's probably the type of person who doesn't like waiting for it."

Daron sighed out loud. "I'm going."

"Figured you might. Call me if you need anything."

"Will do."

Daron climbed into his truck and headed down the drive. On the way to Emma's, he told himself it was nothing personal. He was doing the same thing he'd been doing for the last few years, keeping his promise to Andy.

But he wasn't good at lying, not even to himself. Something major had shifted. For the last three years he'd kept her solidly in the category of "client." He'd managed to keep his professional distance.

He'd blown it the day he kissed her.

Big-time.

Fifteen minutes later he was pounding on Emma's door. She didn't answer. Art opened the door looking a little worse for wear and none too happy. The older man stood on the inside of the screen door and glared out at Daron.

"Is there a reason you're pounding on my door, Daron McKay?"

"Sorry, Art. Boone told me about Emma's truck breaking down. I wanted to make sure she's okay."

"That's a lot of pounding for a blown engine. She's out in the field. One of her mama cows didn't come up at feeding time. I offered to go with her, but Jamie is sleeping and Emma seems to think I need my beauty rest. I told her I'm not getting any purtier to look at."

"I'll go check on her."

"Go on with you, then. But you might not want to ruffle her feathers."

"I reckon no matter what, her feathers are gonna be ruffled," Daron said, managing to keep a straight face.

Art chuckled. "You do manage to bring out the best in her."

Art started to cough and Jamie peeked around his legs, her thumb shoved in her mouth. Daron felt a change of plans coming on as the older man doubled over with the force of the cough, and Jamie seemed worried, unsure, her blue eyes filling with tears.

"I have an idea. How about if I stay here with you and Jamie? If Emma doesn't show up soon, then I'll go looking for her."

Art finally managed to catch his breath, but his face was red. "I guess that'll suit, since you don't seem to think we can manage without your help."

"I'm not meaning to interfere, Art."

"I know you're not. Jamie here is supposed to be napping."

Daron picked up the little girl. "Then I'll read to her and maybe she'll go to sleep."

He carried Jamie to the living room and covered her with a quilt. She curled on her side and grinned as she shoved her thumb in her mouth. "Read the princess book?"

"You got it, kiddo." Daron looked around and spotted a horsemanship magazine on the table. "This has pictures and I don't see a princess book."

"I like horses." She closed her eyes. "And princesses."

Art walked through the room, shaking his head.

Daron sat on the edge of the sofa and started to read about a mare that had a good showing at a national event. The horse had been an underdog, not favored to win. The breeding wasn't the best. The training was local and the rider was the owner. But they showed everyone. The page was dog-eared more than once.

He showed Jamie the picture of the horse. She told him it was a bay. He agreed. She knew her colors. He turned the page and showed her another horse. "Chestnut," she said when she saw the pretty red filly. They played "name the color" for a while.

Every few pages he glanced at his watch and then out the window.

Jamie was dozing when the front door opened. He winked at Emma. It was a flirty gesture and probably wasted on a worn-out cowgirl whose braids were coming undone and whose daughter needed heart surgery.

"Boone told you, didn't he?" Emma asked as she stopped in front of the woodstove to get warm.

"He did. Jamie and I have been reading a magazine about horses, waiting for you. Unless you need help. I didn't want to get in the way."

"I found the heifer I was looking for and put her in the corral. She'll probably calve tomorrow. Or maybe tonight. She seems prone to orneriness."

"I have an extra truck for you to use," he said, glancing down at Jamie. She was sound asleep. "If you want, I'll drive you out to get it."

Emma sat down in a nearby rocking chair. Her forehead was furrowed, and after a long moment, she finally nodded. "I want to say I don't need your truck. But that would be my pride talking. I need to be able to work and take care of my daughter."

"Then we'll leave Jamie in Art's capable hands and run over to get the truck." He stood, letting Jamie nestle into the couch as he pulled the blanket up around her. "Will the two of them be okay together for fifteen minutes or so?"

Emma had moved from the rocking chair and she leaned over her sleeping daughter. Lightly she brushed a curl from Jamie's brow. It was easy to see her concern for her child. She didn't have to tell him. He doubted if she talked about it much with anyone. In the next couple of months, though, her daughter would possibly undergo open-heart surgery. It wasn't an easy thing to think about.

"They'll be fine," she said as she moved away from the sofa and the sleeping child. "Let me tell Art where I'm going and I'll grab my purse. If you don't mind, I need to stop by the feed store in Martin's Crossing."

A few minutes later Art was in the recliner in the living room, Jamie was still sleeping and Daron was following Emma to his truck.

"What are you going to do about Pete?" he asked as he pulled onto the road. "He's no longer just a stupid addict looking for money. He's probably involved in things he wishes he could get out of. If he's coming to you for money, he's desperate."

"I don't think he'll hurt us."

"No, maybe he won't. But you don't know who he's involved with. Emma, these people don't care who they hurt. They just want their money."

She covered her face with her hands. "I'm so tired. I'm tired of Pete dragging us into his problems. I'm tired of trying to make everything work for everyone else. I'm just tired."

"I know," he said quietly, giving her a minute to pull herself together.

"I'm fine. I really am. And I'm not sure what to do about Pete. I would really like for life to be simple again."

He pulled into the parking lot of Martin's Crossing feed store and backed his truck up to the loading dock. "I do know."

She turned that dazzling smile on him,

the one he hadn't seen too often. She'd spent more time frowning at him than smiling. He'd gotten on her nerves, always hanging around. Now it seemed as if the two of them had become a habit. She was used to him always being around. He was used to her telling him to go away. But all of a sudden, she wasn't too eager to run him off. And he wasn't too eager to leave.

As they got out of the truck and headed to the entrance of the store, he caught sight of a familiar truck. Pete.

Nothing about this felt right. And leaving Art, Jamie and Emma alone and defenseless, that didn't set well with him. She wasn't going to like it, but her life was about to get a lot more complicated.

Chapter Nine

The truck Daron loaned her was about ten years newer than her old farm truck. It shifted easily, started without pumping the gas and didn't die going up hills. On Saturday morning she drove through the field looking for the cow she'd expected to calve. She parked and got out. There were several head gathered under a tree. She walked the area, checking behind brush.

She found a section of fence that the cattle had ridden down, pushing their heads through to get grass on the other side. After all, it was always greener over there. She headed back to the truck for tools and work gloves. She pounded the posts back into the ground, made sure they were sturdy, then tightened the few strands of barbed wire.

The sound of a cow in distress caught her

attention. She stood still, listening. *No. No. No.* Not the heifer. She hurried back to the truck and drove in the general vicinity she thought the sound came from. As she pulled up to a stand of trees, she caught sight of the black cow stretched out on her side. She was heaving, raising her head to cry out and then heaving again.

"This is not how I wanted this to go, Mama." Emma knelt beside the heifer. "I'd prefer you do this on your own."

She got up and hurried back to the truck, but then remembered, it wasn't her truck. She didn't have her calving jack, gloves or anything else she might need to pull a calf. She did find some rope. She could make do if things didn't happen on their own.

When she got back to the cow, she was heaving, pushing. The calf's hooves were out. The cow looked as if she'd been at it a long time. She was worn slick, too tired to really try.

"Listen, Mama, I understand. Really I do. Twelve hours of labor, all alone. Believe me, I get it. But you've got to get this baby out or I'm going to lose you both. And I don't want that."

Obviously the cow didn't really care what she had to say.

"Okay, you push, I'll get these ropes around those hooves and we'll do this together."

On the next push she got a loop around each hoof of the calf. It wasn't going to be easy without the calving jack to wench the baby out, but she'd done it this way before. It took muscle, and probably more strength than she had. But somehow her adrenaline kicked in. Fifteen minutes later the calf was curled up on the ground and the mama cow found a little energy to clean her up.

Emma sat down on the cold ground a short distance away. She was too exhausted to care that it was damp. She didn't really mind the cold. It was a good morning, watching that new baby get up on her legs, wobble a bit, then find her first breakfast, safe at her mother's side.

A truck idled up. She turned, not surprised to see Daron McKay. He got out of his truck and a few minutes later he was sitting next to her.

"Art was worried." He leaned back to watch the heifer and her baby. "Can't see something like this in the city."

"No, probably not. But it's an amazing thing to see. I'll text Art." She sat a few minutes longer. "What are you doing here?"

"Good to see you, too, Emma." He sat with

his knees up, his arms resting on them, his gaze focused on the cow. "I have a crew at your house, putting new shingles on that section of roof."

She started to tell him he shouldn't have. But the new Emma was trying to be grateful. She'd been praying about it, about allowing people to help her. She couldn't do it all on her own. And Granddad was getting too old. It was time to admit that maybe it was okay to accept help.

Pride was a difficult thing to let go of.

"You're not going to tell me to stop interfering?"

She bumped her shoulder against his and then rested it there. And it felt good. "No."

"That's good. Because there's something else I have to tell you."

"I don't like the way that sounds," she admitted. The calf finished nursing and took a few awkward steps.

"No, you probably won't. But I want you to hear me out. I'm worried about Pete and what he's involved in."

"Me, too," she said.

"I've asked Lucy to stay with you all for a while. Just to keep an eye on things. She's between jobs and she doesn't mind."

A stranger in her home, watching over

them? She bristled at the idea. "I can watch out for my family just fine, Daron."

"I know you can. But I'd feel better if she was here."

"We are *not* your problem. I know you believe you are responsible for Andy's death. You're not. An IED killed him. It injured you and Boone. You don't have to do this."

"I know I don't." He sat there, arms crossed over his knees, and then he slowly looked at her. "I'm doing it for you."

Her heart thawed just a bit. There were dozens of reasons to pull away from him, and only one reason to lean toward him, to kiss him on his cheek. Because he was kind.

So she kissed him and then she stood, because she needed to go to the house, to let her granddad know she was okay. She needed space from this man because he was burrowing into her heart, and she thought that when he left there would be a Daron-size piece of it missing.

"I have to go check on Jamie. We have a doctor's appointment Tuesday. In Austin."

He stood next to her. "I know. When I left she was sitting with Boone telling him all about the Christmas tree and what she wants for Christmas."

"She wants ponies and kittens and puppies." Emma knew the list by heart. "Oh, and an elephant."

"I'd like to see you put that in your barn."

"If I could give her an elephant, I would." She smiled.

"You would give her anything." He laughed. "I would give her anything. I think right now Boone is wondering if he could find an actual elephant."

He opened her truck door for her. She would have hugged him at that moment, but she needed a shower. It was a point in his favor that he would even stand next to her. She wondered what type of women he dated. It was a dangerous thought, because she knew the world he came from. Married to Andy, for a short time, she'd been a part of that world. "Don't worry," he said.

"I'm not. Okay, maybe a little."

"About Jamie?" he asked as he leaned against the open truck door.

"Yes, Jamie. And Pete. Sometimes I even worry about you."

He showed her that dimple in his cheek, the one that could make a girl develop a serious crush. "Now, why would you worry about me?"

Why would she? He was standing there, all

tall and confident in blue jeans and a cowboy hat.

"Because you're still hanging around here instead of moving on with your life."

The dimple deepened, throwing her off-kilter. "Sweetheart, that is where you're wrong. I'm exactly where I want to be. And I am moving forward with my life."

Her heart slammed against her ribs. "Don't say things like that."

"Why not? Unless I mean them?" he asked. His grin disappeared, but the look on his face was just as dangerous. "I mean it."

Then he closed the truck door and walked away.

Daron parked next to Emma. As she got out of the truck, she looked a little worse for wear. It was barely eight in the morning and she'd probably been up for several hours already. Her grandfather had been up since six and he said she'd already been long gone. Jamie had still been asleep when Daron got there, but she'd woken up and was busy entertaining Boone when Daron left the house to go find Emma.

The roofing crew was hard at it. There were four men and he guessed they'd get a big portion of the roof done by evening.

"This is too much," Emma said. "I'm working at being more accepting of help. But a new roof isn't just help."

He walked with her toward the house. "Accept it, Emma. I'm also going to put plastic on the windows. That might help keep the wind out."

"Thank you," she said softly, and he didn't look down. He didn't want to see tears and he doubted she wanted him to see. "I'm going to take a shower and then you can introduce me to Lucy. But really, she doesn't have to stay here."

"She does. And she agrees."

He didn't tell her the rest. He had the police doing some checking on Pete and who he might be in trouble with. Emma left him in the living room. Jamie was showing Lucy a book about elephants and explaining why one would be a good pet. Lucy had never been much of a kid person, but she was softening up, her hand even stroking Jamie's blond curls.

Daron didn't know all of Andy and Emma's story, but he could guess that his friend had done a number on Emma's self-confidence. Andy would have expected a lot. And then there was the fact that he hadn't been faithful. Idiot. He'd been given a gift and he hadn't cherished it.

Daron went to the kitchen and put on a fresh pot of coffee. Art was cooking up some eggs and bacon on the stove. He looked a little run-down but better than he had the previous day.

"Art, I can do that."

Art faced him, spatula in hand. "It's the least I can do, make you all breakfast. We appreciate this. I'd appreciate it more if I knew why you thought we needed a bodyguard."

Daron sat down at the kitchen table and explained. Because Art deserved to know. He had a right to protect his family. Art turned off the stove and removed the pan of eggs from the burner. "That boy needs to be locked up for his own safety."

"Yeah, he does. Unfortunately something has to happen in order to do that."

"I reckon. But I hate that something always has to happen before a person can get help."

"Me, too."

Emma entered the room, her hair damp from her shower. She'd changed into jeans and a pale blue T-shirt, her feet bare. She glanced at him, shy, then went to the coffeepot. She hugged Art before pouring herself a cup.

"We have a new heifer calf," she told her grandfather.

"That's good news. You had to pull her?" Art asked as he scooped out eggs and bacon and handed her the plate. "Jamie had cereal for breakfast."

"Thanks, Granddad." She rose on tiptoe to kiss his cheek. "Yes, I had to pull her. It wasn't too bad. The cow was just worn out and needed a little help. I need to transfer stuff from the old truck to Daron's. I didn't have the jack or gloves."

She sat down across from Daron and raised her gaze to meet his. "Do you want breakfast?"

"In a minute."

Lucy joined them, pouring herself a cup of coffee. "Jamie is drawing pictures of elephants. In case we wondered what she wants for Christmas."

Daron pushed a chair out with his foot. "Join us."

Lucy nodded, but she filled her a plate first.

"Lucy, I don't think you've met Emma Shaw. Emma, this is our partner Lucy Palermo."

Lucy gave Emma a somewhat pleasant look. That was as pleasant as Lucy got. She'd had a rough childhood, even rougher teenage years. She kept to herself, a habit learned from her mother. Don't trust. Don't talk.

"Nice to meet you, Emma. I've heard a lot about you." She shot Daron one of her rare smiles. It looked more like a smirk.

"Nice to meet you, too." Emma set her coffee cup on the table. "You really don't have to do this. I know Daron is worried and…"

Lucy raised a hand to stop Emma. "I'm here because I'm worried, too. This is something we all talked about."

"Maybe I should have been included in this conversation *we* all had?" Emma said with a bit of bite in her tone.

"We're discussing it now," Lucy shot back.

"Good, this is promising." Boone entered the room. "Lucy, we need to get you declawed. Daron, haven't you called the vet?"

Daron laughed and so did Art. At least two of them were on the same side. "I tried, but the VA is backlogged and can't declaw for several months."

"You all are so funny," Lucy snarled, and then she dug into the breakfast. "Remember, I'm armed."

Daron glanced at Emma. "Lucy does love her weapons."

"I'm a good bodyguard and don't you forget it, Daron McKay. I'm more than a pretty smile and flashy gray eyes."

He put a hand to his heart. "Ouch. You got me there. My weapon is my dimple."

Boone sat down at the table with them. "The two of you are like siblings in the back of a van on a long vacation."

"Something Boone knows all about." Daron got up to take his cup to the sink.

"Yeah, if it has to do with siblings, I know a thing or two. But we need to discuss this. I have to put together a crew for a big oil CEO coming to Houston for meetings. Daron, you're staying here to man the office for a week or so?"

"Yes, and to plan for that big conference in January."

"That leaves me here," Lucy said. "I'll be able to help you in Houston if you need me. And if Daron needs me at the office, I can manage."

"I don't need twenty-four-seven protection," Emma tried to protest. Daron wanted to tell her he understood. She didn't want them all invading her life. But for now, this was best. They were all in agreement. They'd served with Andy. They cared about her.

Jamie entered the room, killing any further conversation. She crawled onto her mom's lap and began to draw more elephant pictures. Emma leaned close, kissing the little girl's head.

"This is an elephant with big ears, Mommy." Jamie pointed at the picture. "And it likes kittens."

"So the elephant wants a pet kitten?" Emma asked.

Jamie nodded, her head tucked beneath Emma's chin. Daron leaned against the counter and watched the two of them.

There was definitely no way he was getting out of this situation without losing a big chunk of his heart.

Chapter Ten

Emma hefted a tray of Monday meat loaf specials and headed for table ten. She said a quick hello to an older friend of Art's, side-stepped Ned and managed to get to the table without losing a single plate. She counted that as an accomplishment.

After she'd served the customers, refilled their drinks and chatted briefly, she headed back to the kitchen. Duke was stirring up something chocolate. She wanted chocolate. Badly.

"Have a bite," Duke offered. He grabbed a spoon and scooped her out some. "Chocolate pie filling."

She took it, relished it and tossed the spoon in the sink. "That's amazing."

"Better than cake?" he teased.

"Definitely better than cake."

"About your mare," he said as she headed out of the kitchen.

She paused and then did an about-face. "What?"

She never asked about Bell. She didn't visit. She pretended the horse had never existed because it was easier than giving up on a dream. If she pretended the dream hadn't existed, it hurt less.

"I'm only telling you this because I think you have a right to know. Daron is trying to buy the mare. We told him she's not for sale, because that's the deal we made with you. But if you're okay with the urban cowboy buying her, we'll go ahead."

"I'm not okay with him buying her." She closed her eyes and counted to ten. Twice. When she opened her eyes she was still on the edge of angry. "I don't want him to buy that horse. Not because of his city roots but because of his stupid guilty conscience. I don't want pity gifts. I don't want this. Any of it."

She pulled her apron up to her face and growled into it. Behind her the door opened and Ned chuckled. Emma dropped the apron back into place.

"He's infuriating."

Ned full-blown laughed. "Got to be talking about the urban cowboy. Honey, let me tell you something. Yes, he's infuriating. But he's also a wonderful-looking man. I'm old, but I look at him and thank my Good Lord above for allowing me to at least look. You've got him running in circles after you and you're about to send him on down the road?"

"I don't want his pity or his guilt. I thought we were friends. I can use a friend."

Duke poured filling into a prepared pie shell. "He offered to buy her horse back. I thought I should check with Emma before I made any deals."

"Troublemaker," Ned quipped as she turned in an order. "You knew it would rile her and you love to cause that boy problems. The whole lot of you have been picking on him for about twenty years now. But he's stuck with it. He hasn't left that ranch. He hasn't walked away from his friends. I guess we probably should stop calling him city boy. He's as country as the rest of us."

Duke laughed. "Just with shinier boots."

Emma found her sense of humor. "He does have pretty boots."

Ned snorted. "If that's what you're noticing when you look at him, then I think the two of us need to have a long, long talk."

"Ned, seems like *you* ought to ask him

out." Duke handed Emma a pie. "Ready for the fridge."

"Now, what kind of woman would I be if I tried to take Emma's man?" Ned asked as she headed back out of the kitchen. "Besides, I'm too old to take that road again."

"I'm with Ned. I've already been down that route. I'm fine being single."

Duke gave them both a look and shook his head as he went back to his pies. "You all are trying to out plan God. I remember when I tried that. And one day I turned around and found I had a daughter and that the woman I didn't remember was the love of my life. You never know what will happen tomorrow."

"I hope only good things," Emma said. She could use some good days.

"Surely you don't think the Lord is worried about marrying me off, Duke Martin?" Ned cackled a bit. "That ship done sailed. Not that sweet little Emma here can't believe in second chances."

"I think I'm happily single, too." Emma shot her boss a look. "The horse stays at your place. Yours or Jake's. You are *not* to sell it to Daron."

She walked back into the dining room of the restaurant, and there sat Daron McKay, in the flesh. In the last few days she'd gotten used to his continuous presence. No matter where she went, either he or Lucy followed. One of them always seemed to be at the house, too.

It did make her feel better, safer, to have someone watching over Granddad and Jamie while she worked. Today Lucy had even kept Jamie so she wouldn't have to go out in the cold to Breezy's. Emma knew that was a big deal for the other woman, who had freely admitted she wasn't a kid person.

Not that the two of them had shared their deepest secrets. They talked about the weather, about horses and about what to fix for dinner. Occasionally they touched on the surface of their real lives.

She didn't hold on to any real hope that she and Lucy would be best friends.

Her heart skipped to Daron. Because even annoyed, she was glad to see him. And that frightened her. Relying on him, on anyone, scared her.

Except Granddad. He was her one safety net. He had always been there for her. It wasn't that she didn't believe another person could do the same, it was just more comfortable to rely on her grandfather.

She carried water to the table where Daron sat, alone.

"You asked Duke if you could buy the mare," she said as she set the glass in front of him.

"Duke has a big mouth," Daron said as he picked up the menu. "I'm here to follow you home."

"Good. Wonderful. But the horse isn't included in this bodyguard business. I'm letting you all invade my home, my life, and I'm doing that to keep my daughter and grandfather safe. That doesn't give you the right to interfere in the rest of my life."

He pointed to the seat across from her. She sat down, waiting for his explanation. She didn't look at him. Looking might mean falling. For his excuses. Not for him.

"Art told me how much the mare means to you."

She closed her eyes, wishing it were true. She loved the mare. She was a beautiful animal. She was a hope and a promise. And not at all what people thought. Because she wanted that horse. She wanted the dream.

But not the way it had happened.

"No. Daron, just no. Don't go there. Don't bring this up. Just let it go. I don't want the mare back. She's beautiful and wonderful and I don't want her."

"But Art said…"

Emma stopped him. "There are things Granddad doesn't know. And there are things I'm not going to tell you. Just let it go. I don't want the mare. I want the Martins to have her. Someday I'll have a foal out of her. That will be enough."

She could see the wheels turning in Daron's head, and she wondered how long it would take him to connect the dots. But maybe he wouldn't think about it past today. Maybe he would understand the story was too difficult to tell. Only Oregon knew. That was enough.

"Okay, no mare." He leaned back in his chair. "You know, I'll listen if you ever want to talk."

"I know you will. But for now I have to get back to work. Did you want to order?"

"Nope, I'm just here to follow you home when your shift is over."

She got up from the table, hoping he meant it, that he wouldn't push.

He reached for her hand, stopping her escape. "I'll be at your place early tomorrow morning."

"Why?"

"I'm driving you to Austin tomorrow. For Jamie's appointment."

"You really don't have to."

"I think I do. We'll do chores before we

head out, so Art doesn't have to. And while we're gone, Lucy is going to try and convince him to go to the doctor for that cough."

"I hope she can convince him," she admitted. "I haven't been able to get him to go."

"Lucy can be very persuasive."

Lucy wasn't the only one. But she didn't have a chance to tell him that. She found herself busy for the next hour. Folks working on the Christmas bazaar had finished up for the day and were taking a late lunch.

When she finally clocked out, Daron was still there. Duke had joined him for a glass of tea and a slice of pie. The two were talking horses and the price of cattle.

"I'm heading home now. Duke, I'll see you in a couple of days."

Duke stood. "You make sure you let us know how the appointment goes. And if you need anything at all, just call. We're praying for you both, Emma."

"Thank you, Duke. We appreciate it so much."

Daron got up to follow her out. "I'll be at my place tonight."

That took her by surprise. "Okay?"

"It's closer. In case you need anything."

"We have Lucy with us," she reminded him.

"I know." He shrugged, like it didn't matter. "It will be good to stay at my place. Boone's brother, Jase, has been crashing at the camper. It's hard to pace with him constantly wanting to analyze what might be wrong with me."

"All right, then. See you in the morning."

She almost invited him for dinner. But she didn't. Instead she said goodbye to him at her truck, knowing he would follow her home, then go on to his place.

It was better that way.

Daron fixed himself a bologna sandwich that night and he sat on the front porch to eat it. In the field cattle grazed. His cattle. There were horses, just a few. When he wasn't there to take care of them, the ranch hand, Mack, did whatever was necessary.

He loved the ranch. He'd been raised in the city, but small-town life was what fit him. At least at this point in his life. He didn't mind coming up behind a tractor and poking along at twenty miles per hour. He loved the smell of fresh-cut hay in the field.

In the past few months he'd thought about moving back to the city, but he knew it no longer suited him. He'd changed since his tour in Afghanistan. He didn't want a job at his dad's law firm. He didn't want the committee dinners and society functions that his parents enjoyed.

He didn't mind that they enjoyed their life. He just wanted them to see that it wasn't for him.

He went back inside, where he'd built a fire earlier. After sitting outside, where it was cold, he felt good to sit down in front of it.

He dozed. But in the dark he was running. Jamie and Emma were ahead of him. They were running, too. Emma held Jamie in her arms. He was yelling at them to stop. He ran faster, but he couldn't catch up. The blast came out of nowhere. He couldn't reach them.

He sat up with a start, perspiration beading across his forehead. It had been a dream. Of course it had. He rubbed his face to clear the sleep from his eyes, from his mind. Then he got up.

In the kitchen he drank a glass of water while staring out the window at the darkened countryside. He refilled the glass and downed it again. His heart returned to a normal pace. He pulled his keys out of his pocket, pushed his feet into his boots, grabbed a jacket off the hook by the door and headed out the back door.

Minutes later he was driving past Emma's house. He slowed as he drove past. There was a light on in the living room. Someone else couldn't sleep, either. Probably Lucy. Like the rest of them, she sometimes had nightmares.

A shadow moved near the barn. He slowed, turned and idled back. At first he thought it might be his imagination. But he saw it again, crossing the yard. He turned into the drive and pointed his headlights in the direction of the shadow.

He jumped out and headed toward the woman in the bright beam of his headlights.

"What are you doing out here?"

"I could ask the same of you," Emma quipped. "I thought you were going to stay at your place tonight. In order to do that, you actually have to stay."

He walked with her toward the house. "I couldn't sleep."

She accepted the hand he offered, surprising him.

"Me, either," she admitted. "When I woke up I thought I might come out and check on the new calf. I brought her and the mama up yesterday."

"And they're doing okay?" He wanted to ask if she understood how dangerous it was for her to be out there alone. But he remained silent.

"They're good. Do you want a cup of tea?"

"Might as well, since I'm here. But do you mind telling me where Lucy is?"

"I had her take my bed tonight. She's been sleeping on the couch."

"Gotcha."

He followed her to the house. It was starting to rain. Just a light mist, but already the air felt cooler, more like winter.

The house was quiet, lit only with a lamp in the living room and a light above the kitchen sink. Night sounds settled around them. The creak of the old house, the wind picking up, the patter of rain against the windows. She put the cups of water in the microwave and then stood there until it buzzed. Daron sat at the old table, with a yellow Formica top.

All in all, it felt pretty good to be there in her kitchen. It felt restful, something he didn't often feel. He told her that, and she smiled as she stirred sugar into the cups. When she joined him they were silent for a minute. The tea smelled of cinnamon and other spices.

"Why don't you sleep?" she finally asked, taking a cautious sip of her hot tea.

"Nightmares. Tonight you were there. Right before the explosion I called your name."

Her hand slid across the table and met his halfway. Their fingers intertwined, the peaceful feeling grew. He couldn't remember ever feeling so good about his life, even before the military. But if he ever told her it felt right, sitting in that kitchen with her, holding hands, she'd probably run him off and say something about his guilt.

This wasn't guilt. But it also wasn't the time to tell her what he thought it might be. Which was about the best thing that had ever happened to him.

"It was just a dream, Daron. Here we are, all fine."

"Yes, all fine. With Pete and his friends somewhere getting high and with Jamie needing surgery. It's all fine?" It made him angry and he didn't know why. She was entitled to be fine with her life.

Her fingers tightened around his. "What would my faith be if I didn't trust that God could handle this? Yes, I worry. I am sometimes afraid. But in the end, I have to trust. I can either trust or fall apart. I choose faith."

"I wish I had your faith."

She grinned at him. "You'll have to get your own. Mine is being used."

He laughed, then looked down into the cup of amber liquid. "Yeah, I'll have to find my own. I've been working on that."

"And maybe you can find some peace."

"I'm working on that, too. One step at a time, Shaw. Don't push a guy too hard."

"You have to understand something, Daron. My marriage was over. Andy was not good to me." She bit down on her bottom lip, and her eyes looked damp. "I don't like to talk about him, about what happened. It seems wrong. He's gone and he can't defend himself."

"I know," he answered. His own voice was a little tight. If he could undo her past, he would.

She cleared her throat and quickly swiped at the corner of her eye where a tear had escaped. "It's over. It's in the past. I don't want to go back and relive it again and again."

"Why did you sell the mare?"

She sipped her tea and in the silence he could hear a clock ticking the seconds away. Outside, a coyote howled.

"The mare was an apology gift from Andy." She shrugged and then took another sip of tea before continuing. "We tried to work things out and obviously it didn't work. But I have Jamie and I'm not sorry. She's the best thing he ever gave me. The horse is beautiful. But my daughter is everything to me."

"Yes, you have Jamie. And if I say anything else, it'll just be wrong. I'm sorry."

Daron sat back in his chair, absently rubbing the back of his neck. It was hard to find words when everything he wanted to say would have revealed his feelings for the woman sitting across from him. And she wasn't ready to hear it.

As they sat there in silence, he thought about all the ways he would show her a man could be trusted. He wouldn't let her down. He made that silent promise. Somehow he would be the man she could finally count on.

It didn't slip past his attention that this night mattered. A lot. Maybe God wasn't as distant as he'd always thought. Maybe his faith was more than a box checked off on a military form. And maybe this woman would someday accept what he really wanted to tell her.

Chapter Eleven

They left for Austin at six the next morning. Lucy had fixed them a thermos of coffee. The gesture had been unexpected. She'd also given Emma a quick hug and told her not to worry. Art and the farm would be fine. She'd make sure of it. And Emma should just focus on making sure that little girl was okay.

It was a few minutes before eight when they pulled up to the Children's Hospital. Daron had been silent for some time. Emma had been okay with the silence. She'd needed time to think and to pray. Now she was fed up with the silence. She needed for him to say something.

If she were truly honest with herself, she really needed a hug, but she wasn't going to ask for one.

"Here we are," he finally said.

"Yes, we're here." She bit down on her bottom lip and stared up at the big building, all metal and glass. She wondered if it had paintings on the walls and a doctor who sometimes wore googly eyeglasses to make the children laugh.

"We should go in," Daron said.

"I wish we didn't have to," she said, reaching for her purse and for the backpack with snacks, blankets and stuffed animals. "But the sooner we get it over with, the better."

"Yes, come on, Emma, you're not a quitter. You're David going after Goliath with a tiny pebble and a lot of faith. You're Daniel staring down lions."

"And who else?" She smiled as she quizzed him.

He chuckled. "That's all I've got. You've used up my entire repertoire of famous Bible guys who had faith."

They entered the building, Jamie holding tight to Emma and Daron carrying the backpack. Emma allowed herself a few seconds to think that this was how it felt to be part of a couple. *Relish it, then get it out of your system*, she told herself. It almost worked.

She wanted to relish a little longer. But she didn't have the luxury to feel this way. She had Jamie in her arms and a specialist waiting to tell them what would be their next mountain to climb. Their next battle to win.

But she knew they'd conquer all. She knew it the way she knew if she took a breath there would be oxygen.

The specialist was a woman named Dr. Lee. She had dark hair and warm, almond-shaped eyes. Jamie took to her right away, climbing on her lap, taking turns with the stethoscope. Emma watched, taking in every expression on the doctor's face as she examined the little girl on her lap. She turned to her computer and browsed over the notes, Jamie still on her lap.

After a careful examination, Dr. Lee invited them to walk with her. She showed them the examination rooms, explained the parent policy of staying with their children, eating meals with the children, even helping with their recovery if they needed baths, physical therapy, etc.

She led them to an office and invited them to sit. She then poured them coffee and gave Jamie a juice box and apple snacks.

"I would like to do more tests," the doctor told them, her expression serious. Her gaze settled on Jamie, who was busy eating the apple slices. "We want to do the best thing for Jamie and I would rather not rush to judgment and make the wrong choice for her. So we will let you go home today and I will have my office call you later with a schedule for tomorrow."

"Tomorrow? But we live in Braswell. It's a two-hour drive." Daron rested his hand on her arm and gave his head a quick shake. "Okay. Tomorrow."

Dr. Lee's expression remained neutral. "We do have housing if you need a place to stay."

"No, I have family in town." Daron's hand was still on her arm, keeping her from protesting the assumption that she would stay with his parents. With his parents? The idea of it sent a tremor up her spine.

"Good, because I don't want this to be a hardship." Dr. Lee handed a packet of material to Emma. "This is some information for you to look over. There are two very good options if we decide Jamie needs surgery. Of course there's the more standard open-heart surgery. But there's also a cath lab procedure in which we would go through her neck or her groin. Not so invasive. But of course neither procedure is without risk. I don't want you to worry, because the risks are not what we focus on. We focus on the best way to make Jamie a healthy little girl and to give her a very bright future."

"Thank you, Doctor," Emma said. She stood, shook the doctor's hand and gathered her daughter in her arms.

They left a few minutes later, riding down the elevator in silence. They walked across the parking lot in that same silence. Jamie was now in Daron's arms, her head on his shoulder.

"I can't stay in Austin," she said as they got in his truck.

"You have to." Daron started his truck and backed up. "We can stay with my parents. They have plenty of room. They're constantly calling, wanting me to visit. So they'll get their visit and the bonus of meeting Jamie. They've heard a lot about her. About you both."

That didn't help settle her nerves. His parents knew about her. It was hard to say what they knew or what they thought. She decided to keep her doubts to herself.

"Are you sure they won't mind?" she asked instead of bringing up all the reasons the McKays might not want extra company.

"I'm sure they won't mind."

Two days, staying with his parents. She had a feeling they would mind. Very much.

His parents lived in a gated community on the edge of Austin. The lawns were large, sprawling, fenced. The driveways were long and protected. At the end of one of those driveways, Daron came to a stop. The house in front of them was French provincial with pale, gray brick siding. It was two story with multipaned windows, a double door of heavy wood, expansive flower gardens and a three-car garage.

She hadn't brought extra clothes. Or food for Jamie. She hadn't brought anything they might need for an overnight stay. During the drive, Daron had been on the phone with his parents, so she hadn't been able to tell him that this wouldn't work. She couldn't barge into their home with nothing but the clothes on her back.

"Stop worrying," he said with that dimple, the one that should have distracted her.

"What do you mean, stop worrying? I'm walking into your parents' home, unannounced, with my daughter. We didn't bring anything for an overnight stay. We're almost two hours from home. So you're right—I shouldn't worry."

"Trust me," he said. "There's a mall nearby. We can get what you need for one night."

"Of course." Because she had tons of disposable income.

"Let's go inside. Jamie looks like a girl

who needs a nap. Maybe her mom needs a nap, too."

"I don't nap," she said.

"I don't nap," Jamie repeated with a giggle.

Daron shot her a look as he got out of the truck. When he opened the door for her, he took Jamie and leaned to kiss Emma on the top of her head.

"Like mother, like daughter," he whispered. "Both stubborn."

"I'm not," she said, but humor caught up with her, and she grinned.

"Yeah, you are. Lucky for you, I like my women stubborn."

"I'm not," she started again. She wasn't his woman. He shouldn't say things like that. She tried to object, but she didn't get to because he was leading her up the front walk to the house and the door was being opened by a woman who had to be his mother. Her hair was the same shade of not-quite-blond, not-quite-brown. She had his gray eyes. She had his height. She didn't have his smile.

"Mom." He hugged her. "Good to see you."

"Really? Because your avoidance would say otherwise." Her gaze shot past him.

"This is Emma Shaw and her daughter, Jamie. Emma was married to Andy."

"Yes, I know." She held out a beautifully

manicured hand. "Emma, I'm Nora McKay. It's a pleasure to meet you. We have heard quite a bit about you."

"It's nice to meet you, Mrs. McKay." They walked through the house, and it was even more overwhelming inside than out. The rooms were large with high ceilings. The furnishings and décor were expensive.

And yet Daron always seemed at home when he sat at their chrome-and-Formica table. He didn't seem to mind the green upholstered sofa that Granddad had bought new when they moved in twenty years ago.

She reminded herself that he had a beautiful home of his own but he stayed in a camper on the Wilder Ranch.

"Are you hungry?" Mrs. McKay asked.

Jamie chimed in. "Cookies?"

"No cookies," Emma told her.

Mrs. McKay thawed momentarily and smiled at Jamie. "I do have cookies, but I think you should probably have lunch first. Daron, I'm going to let you take care of things. I have a meeting in the city."

He kissed her cheek. "We'll be fine."

Nora McKay gave a quick nod in Emma's direction. "If there's anything you need, let one of us know."

She left. Emma slumped against the counter of the kitchen and let out the breath she'd been holding.

"She's not a fire-breathing dragon," Daron teased. "And even if she is, I'm a dragon slayer."

Emma stood up straight. Jamie was sitting on the floor playing with the baby doll she'd pulled out of her backpack.

What Emma wouldn't give to be three years old and totally unaware of the world and its problems. What she wouldn't give to go back even a few weeks to the days when Daron McKay was just a nuisance and not her dragon-slaying hero.

Then again, maybe not.

That evening, after a day they could all agree had been long, Daron walked Emma to the room she and Jamie would share for the night. They'd found what she needed at a local department store, then had dinner at a chain restaurant. She and Jamie were both exhausted.

"Do you need anything?" He had Jamie on his hip and an arm around Emma. He pulled her a little closer than usual, and she leaned into him, taking him by surprise.

He held her for just a minute. When she

pulled away, there was a glimmer of amusement in her eyes. "That was nice."

"Yeah, it was," he agreed. Wholeheartedly. "Mind if we try that again? Because I'm not sure if it was real, or my imagination."

"It was just a hug," she teased.

"Yeah, but I think it might have been more."

She moved into his arms and then it was the three of them because Jamie raised an arm and pulled her mommy closer. Yeah, definitely fantastic.

"I'm not sure what we're doing," she whispered against his shirt. "I'm afraid, Daron. Of so many things. I'm not ready for this. I'm not ready to feel. Or to be hurt. I have to focus on Jamie and…"

He stopped her by settling a kiss on her brow. "Stop. You don't have to worry."

Jamie reached for her mom. Emma took her and stepped back from him, moving out of his arms and out of his reach.

"I'm patient, Emma."

She rested a hand on his shoulder. "I know. Good night, Daron."

The door closed behind her. He thought he heard her lean against it and sigh. He smiled and leaned close. "Go to bed."

"I will," she answered. And then he heard footsteps leading her away from the door.

Daron turned to go downstairs and saw his mom waiting for him. She wasn't smiling. That didn't bode well.

"Mom," he said, meeting her at the top of the stairs, and they walked down together. "I was going to talk to Dad."

"He's in his office. She seems like a nice girl."

"Yes, she is. She's been through a lot."

His mom gave him a careful look. "So have you. And as your mother, I don't want you to go through any more."

He followed her into the den, where his dad was sitting, an open computer on his lap. He glanced up at them and went back to work. James McKay loved his job. He loved his family, too. But he knew how to focus better than anyone Daron had ever met.

"Dad." Daron took a seat and watched as his dad closed out a file and shut down the computer.

Daron guessed this was going to be another "you're wasting a good education" lecture. From his mom it was going to be a "don't get involved" lecture.

He might as well start things off on the right foot. "You all know that I'm thirty, right?"

His dad pulled off his reading glasses and set them on the table next to his chair. And just like that, Daron felt sixteen again. But he wasn't. He cleared his throat and looked from one parent to the other, because at thirty, he knew himself a little better than he had a dozen years ago.

"I know you're a man with a law degree and I have a practice that I'd like to keep in the family. It was my father's law firm, Daron." His dad sounded tired. Daron relaxed a bit because maybe this was a conversation they needed to have.

He wasn't a lawyer. He had the degree. He'd passed the bar. But he wasn't going to step foot in a courtroom. Ever. "I do know that. And I appreciate that it means a lot to you to see it stay in the family. I'm happy that I have a sister who is interested in the law. I have a business of my own. Someday I might have a son," he said. "And when I do, I'm sure I'll want him to follow in my footsteps. But I would also accept that he might want to find his own path."

Nora McKay smiled. "What you're telling your father is no, thank you?"

"I'm telling him that I'm not a lawyer. That doesn't mean I can't help you out from time to time. I can help manage the business. I can provide security, should anyone need it. But I'm not a lawyer."

"Are you a rancher now?" his dad asked. No sarcasm, which was a good thing.

"I think I might be. And that's the last question I want to answer. For now."

His mom watched him closely. She'd made it a habit, watching him. As if she thought he might lose it one day, no warning, just go crazy.

"I'm fine," he said to her without her having to ask. "I'm happy where I'm at. I have good friends in Braswell. It might not be what you wanted for me, but it's where I am and I'm good."

"And Emma?" his mom asked simply.

"That subject is off-limits."

"We only want the best for you," his mom said as she stood to leave the room.

"I know you do, Mom." He stood, also. "And she's the best thing for me."

She gave a curt nod and left them alone. His dad motioned for him to push the table between them.

"Chess?" his dad said.

"I'll beat you."

His dad smiled. "Yes, you usually do. So how's the business?"

"Good. New clients, repeat clients, exactly what you'd expect it to be. It's keeping the three of us busy and we have a good team that we call when we need extra people on a job."

"I guess you're going to make a career of it, then?"

"I guess I am."

His dad moved his first piece. "Still sleeping in Wilder's camper?"

Daron moved and then he sat back in his chair. "I'm starting to move back to the ranch."

"Really? What changed?"

What had changed? It was simple. A little faith. And a woman who made him fight through the nightmares.

"A lot," he answered. And left it at that. His dad was a brilliant lawyer. He could read people. He knew if someone was guilty and he knew if someone was lying to him.

So any question he asked, he probably already knew the answer. The real question was, did Daron know?

Everything good that had happened to him in the last few years was connected to a woman and a child, their faith, their smiles.

It was unsettling that they meant so much to him, had probably meant that much for some time, and he was just now figuring it out.

Chapter Twelve

It felt good to get home. Even though home meant sharing space with the ever-serious Lucy. Emma sat at the table across from Granddad. Lucy walked into the kitchen but paused. Emma motioned for her to join them.

"You're not bothering us," Emma said. "We're just talking about the visit to the hospital."

"How'd it go?" Lucy asked as she sat down with them.

"They've put her on vitamins and another dose of antibiotics. They're going to let us get through Christmas and then they want to do the procedure. They did several tests and realized they can do a catheterization rather than open-heart surgery. They'll go up through her groin and close the hole with a special mesh device."

"And that will work? I don't know how they can get anything through the veins of a girl that little." Granddad wore his super-skeptical look.

"They can do it." She placed a hand over his. "We're going to worry, but we're also going to have faith. We've gotten through everything together."

Lucy stood abruptly and excused herself.

Granddad waited until he heard the door close. "That young woman has a lot on her mind."

"Yes, she does. I'll go check on her. If Jamie wakes up, you can yell for me."

"I think if that little girl wakes up, she and her old granddad will be just fine. You go tend to Lucy."

Emma walked out the front door, pulling on a jacket as she went. She didn't have to go far, though. Lucy was sitting on the edge of the front porch, the dog, Rascal, next to her. Emma sat down next to her. The dog moved and sprawled on Lucy's lap so that his front paws could rest on Emma's legs.

"This dog is an attention hog," Lucy said in her normal brusque manner.

Emma would have been put off by the tone if she hadn't gotten to know the woman.

Lucy hid kindness beneath her tough exterior. "Yeah, he is. You okay?"

"Hmm, oh yeah, of course." She ran a hand down the black-and-white coat of the border collie. "I'm good."

"Right. Because you didn't act at all upset in there."

"No, not at all." Lucy shot her a look. "You get under a person's skin, Emma. You have to remember. I'm not here to talk feelings with you. I'm here to keep you safe."

"Of course. But you can't spend this much time with someone and not think of them as a friend."

Lucy laughed. "Oh yes, you can. I've spent a lot of time with a lot of different people, and I can't say that I ever wanted to be friends with them."

"Okay, I was wrong."

Lucy sighed. "No, you might be right. But I'm not someone who shares my life. Not with anyone."

"I see. But if you ever want to talk…"

Lucy moved the dog over and got up. "If I was going to talk to anyone, I would talk to you. But don't let that go to your head."

"Never."

"And there's my backup for this evening. I have to drive up to Stephenville to check on my mom." Lucy indicated the Ford truck pulling into the drive. Daron's truck.

"I think we'd be fine on our own for an evening," Emma protested as she watched him getting out of his truck. He stretched, rubbed his lower back, then climbed up in the bed of the truck and grabbed a couple of boxes.

"I don't think he's taking no for an answer," Lucy said as she walked back into the house.

Emma picked her way across the yard, avoiding puddles left from that afternoon's rain. "I didn't expect to see you so soon."

He hopped down from the bed of the truck and grabbed the boxes he'd set on the tailgate. "Lucy needs some time off. I brought a few things."

"It looks that way. What did you bring?" She picked up a third box that he'd left on the tailgate. "What's this?"

"That's the nativity. These are decorations and lights. I thought we'd do something to get in the spirit of Christmas."

"What, you think I have no Christmas spirit?" she asked as she led the way to the house. "I happen to have plenty of Christmas spirit. And decorations. I just haven't put them up yet."

"Thus my spare tree and decorations. I

can't sit in a house with no lights and no tree. I kind of guessed your stuff is in an attic and I don't want to climb up a ladder. So here I am, with everything needed to make this house look like an elf threw up on it."

"Since you put it that way," she joked, opened the door and motioned him inside. "Try to be quiet. Jamie is sleeping."

She was wrong about that. Jamie was definitely up. The minute she saw Daron, she ran across the room and attached herself to him. He put the boxes down and picked up the little girl.

"We're going to decorate a tree this evening. And I brought fried chicken from Duke's, so no one has to cook."

He was thoughtful. Emma knew that, but each time he did something like this, it became more obvious. He was touching their lives in sweet little ways.

Granddad grabbed up the bag from the grocery store and headed off to the kitchen with it. Jamie started looking through an open box that contained store-bought decorations and small plaster figurines to paint. She picked up a tiny star and followed Art from the room.

"This was really nice of you," Emma said as he pulled out a small tree that just had to be shaped and fitted together.

"Nice?" He arched a brow. "I thought it was sweet. The kind of thing that makes a woman swoon."

"Is that what you're going for, swooning?"

"Maybe a little." He said it with a tone that might have been hopeful or teasing.

"Well, I'm not one to swoon. The last time I did, there was no one to catch me."

"I'll catch you," he whispered. He leaned in close, grazing her cheek with a feathery kiss.

"No." Suddenly she was afraid. Because what if he didn't catch her? What if he thought she was the woman he wanted in his life but then realized she didn't fit?

"Stop thinking," he warned. "I can see the wheels turning in your head, and I think you're wrong."

"What if I'm right? What if this is temporary? What if one day we're at a family dinner or a social gathering, and you look across the room and you realize that you made a mistake?"

"That won't happen."

She shook her head. "You don't know that."

"No, maybe I don't. But I want to try this, Emma. I want you to try."

Jamie returned from showing Art her tiny treasure. Emma knelt next to her daughter and admired the star.

"Do you want to paint it? With pretty yellow paint and sparkles?" Emma asked.

Jamie nodded and dug around in the box for the yellow paint. "I can paint it."

"Yes, you can. And we'll write your name on the back so you'll always know that you painted this yourself."

Jamie smiled up at her, big eyes and soft curls. "I like to paint it. Daron paints it, too."

"Do you want me to help you paint?" Daron asked, finding another paintbrush in the box.

They were gathering supplies for painting when a shot vibrated the air and glass shattered. Daron grabbed Emma and Jamie and pushed them to the ground, covering them with his body as another shot rang out. From the kitchen, Art said a few choice words.

"Granddad, are you okay?" Emma called out. She pushed herself out from beneath Daron, but he held tight.

"Don't move." His arms keeping them close.

"Daron, you have to let us up. We have to check on Granddad." She turned in his arms, brushing her hand across his face. "We're safe."

"I know. Just give me a minute."

"This isn't a nightmare, Daron," she said.

"I know. Believe me, I know." He was still

holding her, holding Jamie. He moved, taking them with him, half dragging them to the kitchen.

Art was sitting on the floor, holding a towel to his thigh.

"Granddad, you're hurt. They shot you."

Art shook his head. "I think it's just glass from the kitchen window. They ruined my pants."

She laughed until she stopped wanting to cry. Pete had done this. She wouldn't have believed he would do something like this to her, to his niece.

She heard Daron on his phone, calling 911. He kept them in a corner, protected. Safe.

Daron stood to the side, watching the road, the field, as paramedics loaded a very upset Art into the ambulance. Boone stood nearby, also watching. Just in case whoever had done this came back. Daron didn't think they would. This was a warning. He didn't know what the warning meant, but he knew that he wasn't walking away from Emma and Jamie.

Emma stepped close to his side. He kept his attention on the surrounding area. Without speaking she pushed a piece of gauze to his cheek. He flinched at her touch and she lightened the pressure.

"You're bleeding," she finally said.

"Just from glass. I'm fine."

"We're all okay." She pushed the gauze into her pocket and unwrapped a bandage. "Stop thinking this is your fault."

He let her tend his wound, which was nothing more than a scratch, really. "Is Jamie sleeping?"

"Yes. She's with Kayla. Boone brought her, in case we needed her."

"That was good of him." Daron moved his eyes away from the horizon, just briefly, to look at the woman standing next to him.

She was small, but strong. Her dark hair was pulled back in a ponytail and she wore fuzzy slippers with her jeans and flannel shirt. He wanted to pull her close, inhale the scent of her hair and just hold her. Man, he really wanted to hold her.

But wasn't that what had gotten them in this position? He'd lost focus. He'd been living some strange dream, decorating Christmas trees and baking cookies. Now there were shattered windows and glass everywhere. The Wilder brothers were boarding up the windows. Getting new windows put in would have to wait until tomorrow.

"Pack a bag for each of you. Art will need a few things, too. I think they might keep him overnight, but he'll need clothes when he leaves the hospital tomorrow." He gave the order as she stood there, brows drawn together, probably trying to figure him out.

"Why would we need a bag?"

He glanced down again, this time getting lost for a moment in her dark eyes. The anger flashing in those dark eyes helped him get back on track.

"Because you're staying at the Wilders' for a while."

"We can't stay at the Wilders'. They don't know us. And I'm sure they don't have room for three more. That's ridiculous."

"It isn't ridiculous. Tonight someone shot at your house. If we'd been standing two feet to the right of where we were, if Art had been standing in front of the sink..." His voice shook as he drew the picture for her. "Someone could have been killed tonight."

The color drained from her face and she wobbled a little. He put a hand on her elbow to steady her.

"But Pete wouldn't do that. He wouldn't try to hurt us. He wants money, but he isn't mean."

"Meth changes people. And it isn't just

Pete. It's whoever Pete is in debt to. My guess is Pete owed money, so they bargained with him. If he would deal for them, they'd forgive his debt. Or give him a discount. And then he probably spent the money he made rather than turning it over to the boss."

"How did he get messed up with this business?"

Daron shrugged. "Good people get involved in bad stuff, Emma. That's how life is."

"Yes, I guess. I just wish there was a way to help him."

"He could have gotten you killed. There are people willing to hurt you to teach him a lesson."

"I know," she said, her voice soft and tremulous.

He didn't want her afraid. He wanted her fighting mad, willing to stand her ground. But he wanted her safe, too. "It isn't forever. We'll figure out who Pete is connected to and we'll get rid of them."

"I wish we could get Pete some help."

He still had hold of her arm. "Yeah, me, too. But first things first. Let's pack those bags. And tell Art you'll see him at the hospital."

She peeked into the back of the ambulance,

where Art was arguing that it was only a flesh wound and he didn't need to go to the hospital.

"Art, you have to go." Emma patted his foot and he howled. "Just a flesh wound?"

Art grimaced, eyes narrowed. "I didn't say it doesn't hurt. I just said I don't need to go to the hospital. And I don't want you there, either. Stay home with Jamie."

Daron stepped in behind her. "She's not staying here, Art. You don't have to worry."

"That's good. Don't let her come to the hospital. Boone already said he's going to follow the ambulance. I reckon once I get there, they'll give me something to make me sleep. No reason for Emma to drag Jamie there." Art leaned back on the stretcher. "Now go, so they can get me outta here."

Before he could stop her, Emma was in the ambulance next to her granddad. She leaned over him, kissed his forehead and told him she loved him.

Art patted her arm and told her she could save all of that nonsense for his eulogy, and he doubted he'd need one of those for another twenty years or so.

Daron helped her down and they watched as the ambulance pulled away. "Let's get you packed."

"Why do we have to do this?" she asked as they went inside to throw a few things in suitcases.

Daron zipped up the bag she'd packed for Jamie. "We have to do this because we don't want anyone else to get hurt."

"Right," she agreed. "It just makes me mad. This is my home. I don't like to be run off by thugs."

"I don't like it, either, but there's not much we can do. You can't have Jamie here. It isn't safe."

"I know. It just makes me angry. I'm going to pack our bags."

"I'm going to check the livestock and put a leash on your dog. I'll take him to my place and keep him in the kennel."

"Are you sure?"

"Yeah, I'm sure."

An hour later they were pulling up to the camper he'd called home for the last few years. Boone's big old collie was on the front porch. There was a light on inside.

"You're sure they're expecting us?" she whispered. Jamie was sleeping in the seat next to her.

"Yeah, and let me tell you, the Wilders know

how to show hospitality. If you haven't met Maria Wilder, Boone's mom, you'll love her."

"I'll owe her."

"She won't see it that way." He carried Jamie. Emma followed.

The door of the RV opened as they stepped onto the porch. Lucy motioned them inside.

"You were going to see your mom," Emma said.

"Yeah, you know how to create excitement." Lucy teased, an unusual thing for her. "There's food in here. Mrs. Wilder stocked the fridge. There are clean sheets on the bed and one of the sisters—I can't remember her name because Boone has too many siblings—came down and cleaned the place up a bit."

She stepped aside so Daron could carry Jamie down the short hallway to the bedroom, such as it was. It was a small room, big enough for a bed and a built-in dresser and closet. Jamie didn't stir.

Emma watched from the doorway; then she moved back down the hall to the living area. She sat on the sofa and just stared.

He knelt in front of her and took her hands in his. The door opened. Lucy left.

"It's going to be okay."

"I know. I really do. I don't have a clue what God is doing, but I know He's doing something." She squeezed his hands and then lifted them, kissing the knuckles of one and then the other. "The storms make us appreciate the calm."

"Yeah, this is a crazy storm we're mixed up in."

"It seems like that's what I do best, getting you mixed up in my storms. I'm sorry."

"Don't be. I've found some peace in this storm. Maybe a little faith."

Her eyes watered and he groaned.

"Don't cry. Please." He leaned forward, caught her mouth and kissed her sweetly.

"I should cry more often," she whispered. Her lips brushed his again.

"Yeah, and I should leave because staying here with you is dangerous."

"Thank you. For being there tonight. For protecting us."

He stood, his back tightening in response to the treatment he'd given it the last few hours. She noticed and stood up, too. Her arms went around him and she moved her hands to his spine working out the knots. He leaned in.

"I have to go," he repeated. She rose on tiptoe and touched her lips to his.

"Yes, you do."

The door opened. They broke away from each other. Lucy laughed, unapologetic.

"Should I sing about two little lovebirds, caught kissing in a tree? K.I.S.S.I.N.G. First comes love, then comes—"

"Stop," Daron growled at his partner.

She snickered and headed for the fridge.

"I'll see you tomorrow." He kissed the top of Emma's head, then shot Lucy a warning look.

He left, but he didn't go far. He backed his truck out of the drive and went a hundred feet down the drive. He parked and pulled a blanket out of the backseat.

He trusted Lucy, but he didn't trust Pete. He didn't trust drug dealers who were desperate. He had let Emma down once. On a dusty street in Afghanistan he hadn't been able to save Andy. Tonight he would make sure he didn't let anyone down.

Chapter Thirteen

Emma got up early the next morning. She sat on the front porch of the camper. The only chair was an old lawn chair. It wasn't comfortable, but it served its purpose. As she was sipping her morning coffee, she spotted the truck just down the driveway from the camper. The white King Ranch was parked off in the grass.

She wrapped the blanket around her shoulders, picked up her coffee cup and walked down the driveway. Daron was asleep in the backseat, head against the side window, a small pillow under his cheek. She rapped on the window and he jumped, wiped his mouth and then came fully awake.

"You are an idiot," she said through the glass.

"I thought you knew that," he mumbled.

"I did, but this confirms it. I'm perfectly safe with Lucy, and if she thought you didn't trust her, she'd probably shoot you."

One side of his mouth quirked up. "Yeah, probably. I'll be over in a second for coffee."

"There's a fresh pot. I was going to make biscuits and gravy, but Lucy is making breakfast burritos."

"Gotcha."

"I'm calling Andy's parents today. I think they need to know about Jamie *and* about Pete. I've prayed about it. I have to forgive them. Even if they continue to reject us, I have to forgive."

He pushed open the back door of the truck and climbed out. His curly hair was all over the place and he brushed a hand through it to settle it into place. She wanted to help but resisted the urge.

"I think that's a good idea." His voice was still husky from sleep. His eyes were soft.

"I'm going. If you want breakfast and coffee, come on." She started walking back toward the camper.

"I'm coming with you." He caught up with her, his arm sliding around her waist.

It felt perfect, the two of them on that gravel driveway, his arm around her. But perfect, she knew from experience, could fade into something altogether different. She forced her mind elsewhere. She didn't want to think bad thoughts about him. She didn't want to relive the past.

"So this is where you stay. Even though you have a perfectly good house to live in," she said.

He glanced down at her, questions dancing in his eyes. But he went with it. "Yeah, this is where I stay. When you meet the rest of the Wilders, you'll understand."

"I've met Boone's dad. And his brother, Jase. I think a sister. I'm not sure which one."

"There are a few of them. They're all good people."

"So are you."

She slid from his grasp and walked up the steps of the camper. He followed.

Lucy was fixing Jamie a plate, and Jamie was telling her a story about the kitten she wanted for Christmas. Apparently, if she couldn't have an elephant this year, it would be okay. She could get one next year.

"Daron." Jamie's eyes lit up. "Lucy made burritos."

"I didn't know Lucy could cook." Daron helped himself to an already-made burrito and then poured himself a cup of coffee.

"If you all are okay, I'm going to go ahead

and make this call." Emma poured herself another much-needed cup of coffee. "When I'm done, I'm going to head to Braswell to see Art."

"I'll drive you," Daron offered.

"That would be good." And then she walked outside, unsure and more than a little nervous. With unsteady hands she dialed the number for Andy's parents.

After several rings Mrs. Shaw answered. Loretta. Emma had never called her mother-in-law by her first name. Loretta Shaw had never invited that familiarity. In the beginning it had been all right. She'd had Andy's support. Or believed she had it.

"Mrs. Shaw, it's Emma."

There was a long pause. "Emma. What do you need?"

Hesitant, Emma continued. "I wanted to let you know that Jamie is having surgery. The first week in January."

"I'm sorry to hear that."

"She's your granddaughter. I know this is difficult, but I..." She resented Andy for what he'd done to her. Emma resented the Shaws for their lack of support. But she would never resent her daughter. "I thought you might reconsider. But if you don't, I want you to know the door is always open for you to contact me and see her."

"Andy was very clear, Emma. He told us that Jamie isn't his."

The pain of that betrayal hurt worse than everything else Andy had done.

"He lied, Mrs. Shaw." She'd never been so blunt with any of the Shaws, but she was tired of being accused. "I'm not sure why Andy lied. But he did. Jamie is your granddaughter, and on the eighth of January, just a few short weeks away, she's having surgery. A very serious operation."

"Thank you for letting me know."

"Mrs. Shaw, there is one other thing."

A long sigh could be heard from the other end of the line. "What is it?"

"You might not be aware of this, but Pete needs help. He needs a good rehab program. He's dangerous, Mrs. Shaw. Last night someone shot through our house. Pete threatened me. He's been stealing from us."

"I don't want to hear any more of this." Mrs. Shaw sobbed and hung up.

Emma became aware of Daron standing on the porch with her. "She hung up."

"You have to understand, she doesn't want to hear that she's already lost one son and the other is probably on his way to prison." Daron leaned against the porch rail while she sat on the lawn chair.

"Of course she doesn't. I don't blame her. But if she'd listen, maybe they could get him some help."

He nodded, took a sip of his coffee and stared out over the fields. "It's beautiful here. When I first got back to the States, I couldn't imagine being anywhere else. I wanted to spend my life on the porch of this camper."

"I can see why," she said. "Standing here, it's hard to believe there is anything other than good in the world."

"I think standing here taught me that there still is good in the world." He pulled truck keys out of his pocket. "I have an appointment this morning."

"We're fine. I'm going to see Granddad. We'll probably head home after he's released."

"No, you'll head back here. I want you here, where I can keep you safe. I'd prefer that you don't tell anyone where you're staying. And stick close to Lucy."

"Daron, I don't want this to be my life. And I don't want my relationship with you to be one where you feel obligated to keep us safe."

"I don't feel obligated. See you later." He

took the few steps and looked back up at her when he reached the bottom. "The Christmas bazaar is this weekend. If you and Jamie would like to go, I'd love to take you. Not because I'm obligated, but because I want to spend time with you."

He didn't give her a chance to answer. She watched as he walked down the driveway to his truck, and her mouth pulled up at the corners.

Boone rode with him to Jake Martin's. "Tell me again why you're going to look at Jake's livestock? Because I'm confused why a man who never stays at his own place is suddenly interested in putting a few head of horses on said acreage."

"None. Of. Your. Business," Daron answered again. "Sometimes I wonder why I keep you around."

"I'm worth more alive?" Boone shot back. "Or you would be lonely without me."

"I'm not sure either of those fit."

"Back to horses."

"I told you I plan on staying here. I do plan on living on that ranch."

"Gotcha. Mystery solved. This has something to do with a woman."

Daron hit the brakes and pulled to the side of the road. "Get out."

Boone pointed to himself.

Daron repeated it. "Get out. Your happy-in-the-morning self is about to get on my last nerve. Out."

Boone laughed, and then soon they were both laughing. "Touchy, aren't we?"

"Yeah, I guess I am."

"O love, how hath thou changed the man."

"Don't, Boone."

"Buying a woman a horse is almost as serious as buying her a ring. You realize that, don't you?"

"I didn't say I'm buying her a horse. When did you get so nosy, like someone's cat lady neighbor with binoculars?"

"But I'm right, aren't I? And you have to understand, this is commitment. For a guy with self-diagnosed commitment phobia, this is big. It's almost like we're going to pick out a diamond for her."

"Yeah, I realize it."

Boone openly laughed at him. "This is great."

"I'm glad you're so amused." Daron kept driving, keeping his lips firmly in a straight line. He wouldn't show his amusement. Not to Boone. It would be the same as exposing weakness to a predator.

"Let's discuss this situation with Pete. Do you think he was messed up on drugs and took the shot? Or do you think it's his friends? Business partners. Whatever you'd like to call them."

"I think it's the business partners. Pete's messed up, but I don't really believe he'd hurt Emma and Jamie."

"Meth changes people, Daron. You know that."

"Yeah, I do."

They'd lost classmates to the drug. Good, smart people who made the wrong choices, tried something they couldn't untry.

"The police have a lead or two. It would be good if they could get Pete to testify." Daron turned onto the drive that led to Jake Martin's place.

When they pulled up to the stable, Jake was waiting. He had a little girl hanging on his leg, holding tight as he walked. She was giggling and having the time of her life.

"Pardon me, gentlemen, but this little nugget insists on coming to the barn with me. She says to help, but usually we manage to get a lot less work done when we're together.

Mainly because instead of working horses, we chase kittens."

"You wouldn't happen to have any kittens you want to get rid of, would you?" Daron asked as they headed into the barn. "Or an elephant."

Jake gave him a sideways look. "I'm not even sure how to respond to that. I thought you were here for a horse, and I'm all out of elephants. Only a kid could get a man to ask a question like that. Or get him to consider kittens."

"Do you have any kittens or not?" Daron asked again. This was getting complicated. He no longer felt like himself. It was his face in the mirror, but someone else taking up residence on the inside. Someone who cared that a little girl wanted kittens and elephants. Someone who cared that a woman had given her heart and had it rejected by the man who should have cherished her. He'd given her a horse as a last apology and parting gift.

"Slow down, partner," Boone said in a low, easy tone. "You're here to buy a horse, maybe get a kitten, so why do you suddenly look like you could hurt someone?"

"Sorry. I'm good. So, where is the horse Emma Shaw sold you?" Daron asked Jake.

He'd picked up his little girl. She was now on his shoulders, his hat on her head.

Daron wanted that. He wanted a little boy that looked like Emma, with her dark hair and dark eyes. Or a curious little girl who would be Jamie's best friend.

"She's out here. She foaled a few weeks ago. Best-looking little dun we've ever had on the place. Nice colt."

"Would you sell him?" Daron asked as they walked back into sunshine, the pasture stretching out in front of them. A couple dozen head of horses grazed in the early-morning sunshine.

"I might be tempted to. Next fall, maybe. What is it you're looking for exactly, McKay? Do you want horses for yourself or for Emma? I know she doesn't want that mare back. When we bought the horse she told us she loved the animal but she just couldn't look at her."

"Yeah, she has reasons."

"I'm sure she does," Jake said. "I have a nice bay mare. She's four. I have a two-year-old gelding that shows a lot of promise. I guess it depends on who and what you want the livestock for."

"How much for both?" It was a start.

Jake set his daughter back on the ground

and took his hat off her head to place it back on his own. He named a figure. Boone whistled. Daron pulled the checkbook out of his back pocket. "Sold, if you'll throw in one of those kid ponies I know you raise."

"My POAs don't go cheap, McKay."

Daron didn't doubt that. But a Pony of America seemed the perfect horse for a little girl. Not too small, good disposition. A horse she could grow into.

"Looks to me like nothing around here goes cheap, Martin. You just robbed a man without a weapon. The least you can do is throw in a spotted pony."

"I've got one. He's about ten. Good as gold with kids. I bought him last year, but he doesn't show well and the girls all have horses."

"Package deal?" Daron continued. "Oh, and a kitten."

"The kittens will be ready to go in the next couple of weeks. Pick one today and I'll make sure it's delivered."

"For Christmas?" Daron smiled down at Jake's little girl. Melody, he thought her name was.

"Yeah, for Christmas. You drive a hard bargain, McKay."

They left and Boone managed to stay silent until they were driving down the road.

"That's a mighty big diamond ring you just bought, partner," Boone drawled with a chuckle as punctuation.

Daron didn't respond, and kept on driving. But it got him thinking. About rings. He guessed if this was a marathon, he was miles ahead of Emma in his thinking. He'd just bought her horses. She was still trying to push him away.

He knew he needed to slow down. But he'd never been good at waiting. But he had a feeling if he didn't pull back on the reins, she'd show him the exit real quick.

Chapter Fourteen

Emma came home from work Saturday exhausted and ready for a nap. Lucy looked up as she entered the camper, their "safe house" as Boone liked to call it. Emma paused just inside the door and watched as Lucy helped Jamie hang a pretty star on a tiny Christmas tree.

"Another tree?" Emma said.

"Boone said we'd be here until after Christmas." Lucy swept back her long, dark hair. It was an impatient gesture, but she managed a smile for Jamie. "His mom, Maria, brought down the tree. She said it's not quite two weeks until Christmas, but Jamie definitely needs a tree."

"I'm sure you'd rather be somewhere else? With family?" Emma asked as she kicked off her shoes and headed for the kitchen and a glass of water.

"No, not really. I only have my mom. She's remarried and they usually visit my stepfather's family in California."

"You're not close, you and your mom?" Emma knew better than to dig into Lucy's life. But occasionally she tried.

"We were in the foxhole together for too many years to be close."

"Foxhole?"

Lucy handed Jamie another ornament. "We survived too much together. Blame is a horrible thing. Maybe someday we'll work through it."

"I see. Can I get you something? Coffee, water?"

"No, thanks. I'm going to take a quick walk and get some fresh air. I'll let you help with the tree. Oh, there are gifts to be wrapped."

"Gifts?" She sat down on the edge of the couch. "I haven't been shopping yet."

"I told him no, but he never listens." Lucy stretched. "Oh, and he said he'd take you all later for the daily visit to Art. He said Art is enjoying himself with the Jenkins family."

"It was good of Samantha and Remington to take him in. I bet he is having a good time with Remington's grandfather."

"They're kind of cut from the same cloth. I heard they've been terrorizing the neighbors, shooting bottle rockets at crows or some such. Nothing to hurt anyone, just acting like teenagers."

"I worry about Granddad, but he isn't slowing down much."

"He's a good grandfather," Lucy agreed. "I'll catch you in a few. Boone said to let you know he plans to take you all to the Christmas bazaar tonight."

"I wonder if it has ever occurred to him to ask, not tell?"

Lucy was tugging on her running shoes. "No, I don't think so. Some advice?"

"Sure."

"Stand your ground with him. I know from experience that when he starts getting this way, I play opposites with him. He says go, I stay. He says smile, I frown. It keeps him on his toes. He's a pretty boy who is used to getting his way in all things."

"Thanks. I'll remember that."

Lucy bent to kiss the top of Jamie's head, saluted to Emma and out the door she went. For a run, not a walk. Emma lowered herself to the floor next to Jamie.

"It's almost Christmas. What do you want?

Other than elephants and kittens. Elephants are hard to come by this year."

Jamie giggled. "A giraffe."

"Did someone tell you to ask for a giraffe?" Emma asked.

"Boone," Jamie said. And she reached to hang a pretty globe on the tree. "Boone said tell Daron I want a giraffe."

"Boone is very bad."

"He should be in time-out?" Jamie asked, sitting back with her little legs stretched out in front of her. Her smile was everything good in Emma's world.

Emma pulled her close and kissed her cheeks until she giggled and said, "Stop, Mommy."

Then Jamie kissed Emma's cheeks.

"I love you, Jamie."

Jamie put a hand on each side of her face and leaned close. "I love you, Mommy. And so does Daron."

Emma closed her eyes and leaned in close to her daughter, smelling her sweet little-girl scent and promising herself she wouldn't be broken again. She wouldn't feel less than. She wouldn't apologize for who she was. She wouldn't let a man hurt her. Ever again.

And she would teach her daughter to be strong and to believe in herself. Because little girls should feel cherished and grow up to be young women who valued themselves.

Jamie leaned in and whispered, "Mama crying?"

"No, I'm not." She wasn't. She had weathered the storms of her life and she'd come out stronger. "So, what about Christmas? Other than a giraffe?"

"A baby that pees."

"Not a real one, I hope?" She heard the front door open. Emma looked over the top of Jamie's head at Daron. He was watching them, a guarded expression on his face.

Jamie laughed at his question. "Yes."

"No," Emma said. "But I think we can do a doll. And what, might I ask, is in the bags in the bedroom?"

Daron shrugged. "Stuff."

"We need to talk."

He sat down and waited. "About what?"

"About little girls and how they feel when they really like someone but that person is only in their lives for a while."

"Who isn't going to be around?" he asked.

"Stop, Daron."

"I'm not going anywhere, Emma," he said. He glanced at his watch. "Actually I am going somewhere. I'm going to see Art and then I'm going to the Christmas bazaar. Teddy Dawson has his pony ride set up and I heard there's some pretty amazing boiled shrimp."

"Ponies?" Jamie dropped an ornament in the box, the tree forgotten. She hurried to Daron, crawled up on his lap and gave him a hug.

"You don't play fair," Emma accused.

"Nope. I play for keeps," he quipped. "How long will it take you all to get ready?"

"Fifteen minutes." She gave in too easily. Lucy would have given her a look for that. She hadn't stood her ground. She hadn't said no. She didn't want to say no to Daron in their lives.

When she thought long and hard about it, the only thing she wanted to say no to was him leaving them.

The town green surrounded the Martin's Crossing Community Church. This was where they held the bazaar that brought locals and tourists alike to Martin's Crossing. They came to listen to music, buy homemade crafts, toys and clothes, and eat the many different types of food that a festival such as this one always offered.

"Shrimp?" Daron asked as they wandered through the crowds.

"I have shellfish allergies," Emma told him. "I want a corn dog."

"Corn dog?" He looked appalled. "When you could have anything else, you want a corn dog?"

"Corn dogs are important festival food," she informed him. "They aren't amazing when they're the frozen variety heated up in the oven. But at a festival when they're hand-battered and deep-fried? Amazing."

"Better than a steak sandwich from the VFW guys over there?"

She nodded and kept walking. "You've never tried one, have you?"

"I've had corn dogs."

She arched a brow and waited for him to come clean.

"Okay," he admitted, "I've never had one at a fair. When we were kids, my mom wouldn't allow us to eat carnival food."

"Seriously?" She had to laugh. "Why?"

"They aren't sanitary."

"The hot grease would kill any germs."

He moved next to her in line. "I'm taking your word for that."

"Good. Because I also want a fried Snickers."

He blanched. "Can a human body handle that much grease?"

"Of course it can. And you'll love it."

"If you say so."

She leaned against his shoulder. "You've lived a very sad, sheltered life."

They ate at a picnic table close to a blazing fire pit. The heat felt good. Although it wasn't freezing cold, there was a definite chill in the air. Jamie managed to eat part of her corn dog, then had other things on her mind.

"Can I ride the pony?" she asked Daron, tugging at his sleeve.

"You bet. Why don't I take you, since your mom is still eating? Emma, catch up with us in a minute?"

She nodded and took another bite of fried candy bar.

When she finished she tossed her trash and headed across the lawn to the pony ride. Jamie was on a pretty spotted pony with Daron walking next to her.

Emma stood at the edge of the small fenced enclosure watching her daughter live out her dreams of being a cowgirl. Daron said something and Jamie smiled big. She hoped he wasn't making promises.

A hand clamped down on Emma's arm. She pulled away but the grip tightened. She turned to face the man at her side. Pete. He looked worse. His face was sunken. His hair greasy.

"Emma, you have to help me."

Those weren't the words she expected. Her fear eased a little.

"I can't help you, Pete. You know that. I would like for you to get help, though." She stepped back from him and he released her arm. His gaze shot past her, to someone she couldn't see.

"You can help me. I need money. Andy said he left you a life insurance policy."

"He didn't."

The words were barely out of her mouth when he fled, running through the crowd, pushing people as he went. She turned, knowing Daron must be close. He made it to her side and scanned the crowds. But Pete was gone.

"You okay?" Daron asked.

"I'm fine. He believes I have a life insurance policy from Andy. That's why he keeps coming back. He's delusional."

"Meth does that. It makes people paranoid. It alters the brain's cell structure." He glanced back into the crowd and that was when she realized he didn't have Jamie.

"Where's Jamie?" She panicked.

"I saw Pete with you and I left Jamie with Oregon and Lily."

She released her breath and closed her eyes. "Don't do that to me."

"I wanted her safe."

"I know." She continued to breathe slow and steady, calming her racing heart. "I'm sorry."

His hand rested on her back and he guided her through the crowd. "Should we head back to the Wilders'?"

She nodded. "I think so. We came, we ate, we rode ponies. That's about all the excitement I can take for one night."

But she stopped in a clear area where, for one moment, it was peaceful. There were Christmas lights, a choir in the background singing "O Little Town of Bethlehem" and the nativity near the church. "I love it here. I can't imagine living anywhere else. And even with Pete trying to steal my joy, there is peace." She touched Daron's arm. "Do you feel it?"

He looked stunned, as if he doubted her sanity, but then he nodded. "Yes, I do."

He brushed his thumb against her lips. The gesture was sweet and it caused her to think of how it felt when he held her. When he kissed her.

But she wasn't going there. This thing between them had become tricky. It had opened doors that she'd closed, barred, locked and bolted shut.

"We should go now," she said. Because being with him like this now, this felt dangerous.

Daron sprawled on the sofa in the living room of the camper. Lucy was in the recliner. With Pete's appearance in town last night, he'd decided they should both be on duty. And she'd gotten to the recliner first. That left him tossing and turning all night, and thankful when the sky finally lightened enough to call it morning.

He pushed himself up from the lumpy piece of furniture and made his way to the kitchen and the coffeepot. Footsteps in the hall warned that he wasn't the only one up. He brushed a hand through his hair and went back to making coffee. Emma appeared, looking sweet and sleepy. Her hair was loose, framing her face, making her eyes look large and luminous.

"Do you mind going to church in Martin's Crossing today?" he asked as he poured her a cup of coffee. Then he stuck a couple of slices of bread in the toaster.

"I guess not. Why?" She took the coffee and sat down at the booth-style table.

"I feel more comfortable there. I know the layout and the people."

"Because of Pete?"

"Yeah, because of Pete."

"I don't understand why he can't be arrested."

"No evidence he's committed a crime. He comes to your house asking for money. We could try for a restraining order."

"And what would that do?"

"If he comes within several hundred feet of you, your daughter or your property, he can be arrested. But the problem is, if he's determined, he's going to ignore the order."

"Exactly. Do you think he would just go away? If I had money, which I don't. Would he leave?"

He joined her, sitting across from her at the tiny table. "I don't think so. I think he's like most junkies. He'll go through the money and come back begging for more."

"Yes, you're right," she said softly, then lifted her cup to take a drink. "I really want to go home. Not that this camper isn't lovely, but I miss my kitchen and my space. I miss my cattle."

"We can spend the day there. Maybe take some lunch out there. I had the windows fixed yesterday."

"You shouldn't have done that. I can take care of these things, Daron. It's my house, my family."

He raised his hands, stopping the argument. "I know it is. I know I have a tendency to go full throttle. I just want to make this easier for you."

"But you have to understand, we're not your problem. And I can't repay everything you're doing for us."

He got up from the booth and walked over to the sink, rinsing his cup before facing her again. "I didn't ask you to pay me back. I do know that you're not my problem." He paused, shaking his head. Lucy was in the recliner, probably feigning sleep. "You don't owe me anything. I'm not doing this out of some sense of guilt."

"No?"

"No," he repeated. He looked at the clock on the microwave. "We should get ready for church."

"I'm not going to church," Lucy snarled from the living room. "You know I draw the line at church."

"Yeah, Luce, I know."

Emma had slipped away. He heard the door down the hall close. He heard her talking in soft whispers to her daughter. Jamie giggled, the sound undeniably happy. He guessed the faith of a child was this: heart surgery in the future, not a lot of money, someone waiting to bring harm, and a three-year-old able to giggle.

When they got to church the building was crowded. The pastor told them it was the pre-Christmas rush. Everyone wanted to get in good with the Lord before the big birthday party. Occasional Christians, the pastor called them. They showed up for the special occasions. Christmas. Easter. Daron guessed he kinda fit into that group. His family had been occasional Christians, too. They were good people, his parents. They had a strong marriage. They loved their kids. They just didn't spend much time inside a church.

Maybe they'd had faith, but he didn't remember it getting passed on to him or his sister, Janette.

He watched Emma as she hurried over to hug her grandfather. Daron followed the two of them to a pew they were sharing with Boone and Kayla. He slid in next to Boone. That left Kayla, Boone and Jamie between Emma and him.

He didn't much care for that.

"Do you want to take Jamie to children's

church?" Kayla asked. "I think they're having a puppet play today."

Emma looked down at her daughter. "Do you want to go?"

Jamie nodded, so Emma lifted her and left, squeezing past him to get out. "Want me to go with you?" he asked.

She shook her head. "No, of course not. I'll be right back."

Boone told her where she would find the children's church. She hurried away, talking to Jamie as she went.

Daron glanced at his watch. He would give her four minutes to get there and back.

"She's safe here," Boone assured him.

"I know she is."

He glanced at his watch again. Three minutes. He'd give her one more minute and then he was putting the building on lockdown.

Chapter Fifteen

"You are going to have to give her to me, Emma." The voice came from a doorway on the quiet hallway that obviously wasn't the way to the children's church.

Emma had gotten confused, taken the wrong door. She'd known it and had started back. And then she'd heard the voice. Pete's voice.

He stepped out of the shadows. "I've been waiting, hoping to catch you alone today."

"Pete, don't do this." Emma backed away. She held her daughter against her and tried to calm her as Jamie started to sob. "She's frightened. You're her uncle. Why don't you say hello to her, Pete? She has Andy's eyes. Blue, just like his."

Pete glanced but then looked away. She saw

remorse. She knew she could get to him if she kept talking, connecting him with his niece.

"She's going to be in the hospital in a couple of weeks. You should come visit her. I called your parents. They might come see her."

"I don't think they will," he mumbled. "You're nice, Emma. You just weren't good enough. They wanted Andy to marry someone who fit into his world, not the poor farmer's daughter from Braswell."

"That's mean, Pete." She kissed Jamie's brow and rubbed her back as she held her close. "Jamie is three now. Did you know that? She wants kittens and an elephant for Christmas."

He almost smiled. "Emma, stop. Please stop. You don't understand how much trouble I'm in. I won't hurt her. I'll just spend time with her until that boyfriend of yours can get money from his family. They have plenty. I get that Andy left you high and dry, but it looks like you've bounced back just fine."

"I don't have a boyfriend, Pete. He's just a friend. You know that. He and Andy were friends, so he's checked on us and helped us out."

"I'm not stupid, Emma." He tilted his head, chin up. He was tweaking. Great.

"I know you're not. I'm just telling you that you're wrong."

She had to keep him talking. She knew Daron would notice how long she was gone. He'd come looking for her. Pete noticed her shift to look at the door at the end of the hall.

Before she could stop him, he grabbed Jamie from her arms. From out of nowhere he produced a knife. "Stay here, Emma. Please stay here. Understand that I am sorry, but I have to get money or they're going to hurt all of us."

"Pete, don't do this. You could help the police get these guys. You could do the right thing."

He shook his head and ran down the hall. Jamie was screaming. "Mommy!"

"Jamie, Mommy is here. Don't worry." She let him get a short distance ahead of her and then she ran after him.

He got through the glass door to the outside. Before she could reach it, he jammed something under it so she couldn't open it. She screamed and pounded. He kept going, Jamie yelling for her mommy, the knife hanging loosely in his hand. Halfway to his old truck he dropped the knife and kept going.

Emma watched him drive away. She wanted to know the direction. She pulled out her phone and called 911. As she did the door behind her opened. Footsteps sounded on the tile floor. Daron was yelling at her, telling her to give him details.

Boone was there. Kayla. Granddad. Her world was fuzzy and cold. Numb.

Nothing made sense. Pete had taken Jamie. She tried to explain, to describe. Sobs were choking her, making it hard to talk. But Daron got the details, and after a quick hug, promising it would be okay, he left. Kayla held her tight, promising that if anyone could get Jamie back, it would be Boone and Daron.

"I want to go home," she whispered into Art's shirt a few minutes later. "Granddad, I want to go home. I want to be in my house when they find her and bring her back. I want her to know that we're there waiting for her."

"You got it, kiddo." Art wrapped a protective arm around her and led her through the church. People tried to talk. They touched her arm. They told her they would pray.

As they walked out the front door, Lucy arrived. She pushed through the crowd, positioned herself on Emma's other side, opposite Granddad, and told her to hang tight, that they'd be home in a minute.

A few people followed them to the farm. Boone Wilder's mom, Maria. Duke and Oregon. Remington and Samantha. They sat together in the living room as the police questioned her. They asked the same questions over and over again. She kept answering, trying to remember if she'd left out any details.

"I just want my baby. She's sick," she sobbed. "She has medicine."

Art stood, looking taller and more menacing than a man in bib overalls should look. "I think she's had enough, boys."

The two police officers focused their attention on him for the moment. "Mr. Lewis, we have to question her. That's how we're going to find your granddaughter."

"I understand that, but she's answered all of your questions. She's answered them several times. I don't know what you're hoping to learn from her, but she told you everything. Now I'm asking you gentlemen to back off and let her breathe."

One of them started to rebuke her grandfather. Lucy stepped in. "I think we're all a little stressed. I think you can give the family time to breathe."

The officers stood up. "Mrs. Shaw, we want to find your daughter. We're sorry that we've had to question you this way, but we want every detail so we can find her and bring her home."

She nodded. "I can't think anymore. I just can't. I need to go outside. Lucy, can we go out to the barn? Please."

"Is there something in the barn?" the younger officer asked.

Lucy scrunched her nose at him. "Yes—animals. Fresh air. Space."

"We'll be in the yard, not too far away." The older officer opened the door for Emma and he followed them out.

"Where are we going?" Lucy asked as they crossed to the barn.

"I don't know. I just need to think. I need to breathe. I can't remember everything Pete said. But maybe he gave me a clue. I just have to remember."

"I called his parents. They're on their way. They said they would keep trying his phone."

"That's good of them."

She sat on a square bale of straw next to the barn. It was cool but clear, the sky brilliant blue. Jamie was out there somewhere. With Pete. Or maybe with Pete's dealers. She fought back the panic. "Lucy, will you pray with me?"

Lucy sat down next to her. "I'm not a praying person, Emma. You know that."

"Why?"

"Because my experience with religion

wasn't congregations full of friends and family. It wasn't kind."

"I'm sorry. Do you mind if I pray?"

Lucy stared at her for a moment, then took hold of her hand. "I'll pray with you."

They bowed their heads and Lucy prayed. It was heartfelt, sweet, simple. When she said the final amen, Emma kept her head bowed. She let tears trickle down her cheeks.

Suddenly a hand touched her back. Daron moved in front of her, knelt and took her in his arms.

"You didn't find her?"

"We know where she is. Pete has her in Braswell in an old house. He doesn't know that we know. But I want you to come with us. I want you to talk to him and see if we can reason with him. We don't want her hurt. We don't want to have to hurt him."

"She's in Braswell. Alone with Pete."

"There are people watching the house. They won't let anything happen to her."

"Okay, let's go."

They took Lucy with them to Braswell. Emma sat between Daron and his partner. She closed her eyes, praying that God would somehow loosen up Pete's heart and give him a clear mind. A conscience. Just for a few minutes if he would do the right thing.

The house in Braswell was exactly what Daron described. It was a drug house. Empty with broken windows. Brown weeds covered the lawn. It might have been a pretty house at one time. Two stories with a small front porch. But time and poverty had gotten the best of it. The window boxes were empty. The shrubs were nearly to the roof.

She didn't wait for instructions. When Daron stopped to talk to Lucy, Emma moved to the broken window on the porch.

"Pete, it's me. It's Emma. I'm here to get Jamie. Tell her that I'm here, so she won't be afraid." She peeked inside and saw Pete in a corner, her daughter on his lap asleep. Pete held a finger to his mouth, but it was too late. Jamie stirred, then woke up screaming for her mommy.

"Now see what you've done."

"I'm sorry. But, Pete, you have to take responsibility. You've kidnapped your own niece. You can rationalize all you want, but this is on you. You know that you can make this better or worse. You can hand her over and get help. It's up to you. I want you to someday apologize and do your best to be the uncle she deserves. Be the person you deserve to be."

"They'll kill me if I don't pay them."

"That's something the police can help you with. Maybe you can help the police?"

He kept hold of Jamie, but Emma could see that he was trembling. She climbed through the window and stepped carefully over broken glass. Pete scooted farther into the corner.

"Pete, give me my daughter."

He stood, holding Jamie away from him, toward her, and then he lunged. The bullet hit him in the shoulder, taking him down. Emma grabbed her daughter and jumped back. Jamie was crying. Maybe they were both crying. It was hard to hear. Pete was screaming that he'd been shot. Police were ramming down the door.

Daron was there, gathering them close, telling them they were safe. His arms remained close around them as he led them from the house littered with needles and old clothes. The stench of the place remained in her nostrils as she walked back to his truck.

Lucy wrapped a blanket around her.

"That was stupid, you know." Lucy gave her a serious look and shook her head. "Of all the stunts you could have pulled, that was the worst."

"I had to."

Lucy clucked a few times like an old mother hen, totally out of character. "Yeah, I know."

The police questioned her again. This time she was sitting in Daron's truck and he was next to her. Jamie was in her arms, telling her that Uncle Pete gave her a lollipop and said he was sorry.

As they loaded Pete in the ambulance, his parents arrived. They talked to the police and to their son, and then they waited. For her, she realized. They wanted to see their granddaughter. Emma was both thrilled and frightened.

Daron opened the door of the truck. "Do you want me to send them on their way?"

She shook her head. "No, I'll talk to them for a minute. But then Jamie and I want to go home."

He led the Shaws to his truck. Emma and Jamie remained inside. She watched as he spoke to Andy's parents, people he had known most of his life. She tried to read their very guarded expressions. She wondered if they had ever looked at the cards and pictures she'd sent. Or would today be the first time they really saw their granddaughter?

Mrs. Shaw approached the open door, her husband behind her. Lucy was nearby, her most menacing look directed at the couple. Emma felt her chest loosen, the fear ebbing away.

"Emma. Jamie." Mrs. Shaw wiped at the tears trickling down her cheeks. "My goodness, Jamie, you do look like your daddy."

Jamie didn't speak. She cuddled against Emma and looked at the woman she should have known.

"Jamie, this is your grandmother and grandfather Shaw."

"Uncle Pete needs a time-out," Jamie sobbed, and buried her face again.

Mrs. Shaw cried, "Yes, he does. Emma, I am so sorry. Please forgive us."

"Of course." Emma kissed Jamie's cheek. "We forgive you. We're just very tired right now and we want to go home."

"Of course you do." Mrs. Shaw touched Jamie, the gesture timid. Her hand rested on Jamie's back for a brief moment. "I hope that we can visit. When you're up to it."

"Yes, we'd like that."

Mrs. Shaw hugged both Jamie and Emma before walking away with her husband.

Daron watched the Shaws leave; then he got back in his truck. He sat behind the wheel for a minute before he turned the key in the ignition.

"This has been a long day," he finally said.

"You can say that again," Lucy said from

the backseat. "Emma, you are about the toughest case we've ever had."

Emma laughed a little. He was glad to hear that laugh. It meant she was already bouncing back.

"I'm so tired," she said after a minute.

Jamie, buckled in the seat between them, was already dozing, her thumb in her mouth. Emma leaned close to her daughter. He saw her breathe deep and then touch Jamie's hair.

"The police want us to go by the ER. She should be checked out—just as a precaution." Daron waited until he was actually on the road to the hospital to make this announcement. He guessed that made him a chicken.

Emma gave her daughter a careful look and nodded. "Yes, of course."

The ER staff was expecting them. They had an exam room and Dr. Jacobs was waiting. Daron was thankful it was someone Jamie knew. It made it easier that she knew his smile, his voice. He allowed her to sit on her mom's lap and he talked about ponies and kittens. Daron stood in the doorway, watching over them.

He guessed he'd have to figure things out now. He had been watching over them for the last few years. He'd known for a couple of years that Pete was being a nuisance, so his presence had seemed necessary. Or so he'd told himself.

Dr. Jacobs finished the exam and handed Jamie a big stuffed horse. "I heard you were coming and that you'd had a pretty eventful day, so I went down to the gift shop to see if they had any ponies. This was the only one, but they assured me he doesn't eat much, doesn't make messes and he can sleep in the house."

Jamie accepted the gift, and whispered, "Thank you."

Daron watched as the good doctor said goodbye to the patient and her mother. A new emotion washed over him. Jealousy.

He shrugged and let it roll off. Water off a duck's back, he told himself.

Chapter Sixteen

Christmas morning dawned overcast and cool with flurries falling. Jamie ran out the front door and yelled, "Snow."

It wasn't really snow, but living in Texas Hill Country, they would take what they could get. Emma followed her daughter out, holding a jacket out to slip her arms in. Jamie wiggled into the jacket, then tromped down the steps of the porch and into the yard. She stood for a full minute with her face up and her tongue out. The flurries turned into large white feathery flakes. They were the type that fell hard and fast but then ended as quickly as they began.

Granddad wandered to the door. "You girls are silly. Aren't we going to head over to the McKay Ranch?"

"Yes, soon." Emma tilted her head and

caught a few flakes with her own tongue. Jamie saw and laughed.

Emma wasn't in a hurry to go to Daron's. She was afraid. Of a lot of things. Of what she felt. Of the future. Of spending this day with his family. Old emotions were rearing their ugly head. She wasn't good enough. He didn't really want her, just the idea of her. He'd realize that soon and then she'd be left with a broken heart.

No, she caught herself. Not a broken heart. A heart could only be broken if a person loved someone who hurt them. She didn't love Daron. They were friends. She cared about him. They had shared some sweet moments.

That didn't make it love.

But he'd invited them to spend Christmas with him and his family, and she'd accepted. Partly because she wanted time with him. She found herself missing him now that Pete was in jail and he'd helped the police get the cartel that he'd been working for. She also thought that she would tell him soon they needed time and space because she was afraid they'd been thrown together and that it was possible she was confused about what she felt. Or maybe he was confused.

She knew that someday she would marry again. She didn't want a second failed marriage.

This was her putting the horse before the cart, thinking that there was more to her relationship with Daron than maybe there was. And that was why she had to take a step back and discover the truth. What she felt. What he felt.

Granddad had fixed breakfast that morning. It was a Christmas tradition. Every year he made the same thing for Christmas breakfast. Biscuits and gravy, cinnamon rolls, eggs and bacon. Afterward they would usually tell the Christmas story and then open gifts.

This year Granddad read the Christmas story from the Bible and then they jumped in the truck, Daron's truck, and headed south in the direction of the McKay spread, as her granddad called it.

With each passing minute, Emma's apprehension grew. Her granddad shot her a careful look. "Em, if you don't breathe, you're going to pass out. Calm down. It isn't like you haven't met these people before. It's Christmas, so smile and stop looking like you're heading to the hangman's noose."

She nodded and managed a grimace that was meant to be a smile. She took a few deep breaths and wiped her palms down the sides of her jeans. She looked at the jeans she'd picked, with boots and a long tunic-style sweater. Maybe she should have worn a dress?

Art shook his head. He was pulling up to the house. There were several cars already parked out front. She guessed them to belong to his parents and maybe his sister, Janette.

"We're here!" Jamie said gleefully.

Emma smiled down at her daughter, got out of the truck and they walked hand in hand to the front door of a home that looked more like a lodge and less like a home. A woman about her age answered the door.

"You must be Emma! And Jamie and Art. Please, come in. We're all in the kitchen. Mom doesn't really cook, but she has a great caterer. We brought everything down in coolers. It's amazing."

Emma allowed Janette to lead her through the house to the kitchen. Art was muttering about electric bills and wasted space. She sent him a warning look and he just chuckled and kept on talking.

Standing in the kitchen, Daron smiled when he saw them. Emma froze, trying to fit this man into the image of the one she'd known for several years. This man was dressed in slacks, a soft gray button-down shirt and black boots. His face was freshly shaved. He smelled wonderful, all spices and mountain air kind of wonderful.

He lifted Jamie and then wrapped an arm around Emma. Art was already picking over the food and talking to Daron's dad.

"I want an elephant," Jamie whispered to Daron.

He hugged her tight. "I know you do. I'm afraid the store was all out of elephants this year. I did get something pretty cute, though." To Emma he said, "You look beautiful."

She wanted him to mean it. She wanted him to mean that she fit. That she didn't have to be someone else.

"Have you seen Daron's new horses?" Janette asked as they walked to the living room, where the tree sparkled and presents wrapped in bright-colored paper were piled high.

"New horses?" She shook her head. "I guess I haven't."

"Big mouth," Daron said as he scooted past his sister. "I was going to show you today. One of them needs some work. I bought them from Jake."

"Not…" She bit down on her lip.

He shook his head. "Not the mare. I wouldn't do that. But the mare has a foal. Pretty nice colt."

She shook her head and he gave a brief nod. "You can show me your horses later."

A noise from under the tree offered a welcome distraction. Jamie was scurrying, trying to find it. She grabbed at a blanket and laughed, a real belly laugh, the kind that made a mom so happy. Even if the thing her daughter was laughing at was a living, breathing creature. A kitten.

"My kitty." Jamie dropped to her knees and tried to open the cage. Janette got down on the floor to help her. The kitten was long-haired, gray and had blue eyes. It mewed and, as soon as the door was open, crawled into Jamie's lap.

"A kitten," Emma said. She managed to frown at Daron. She wanted to be upset with him. But the kitten and her daughter made a beautiful picture, and she couldn't be mad. She shifted her gaze from his because she didn't want to be lost in what she felt for him.

"We should open gifts," Nora McKay suggested, watching the two of them and then shifting her eyes away. She started passing around the many presents from under the tree, enlisting Jamie as her helper.

Jamie took the responsibility very seriously, holding her kitten under one arm as she delivered gifts. There was a pile for her, and when all the gifts were passed out, Jamie leaned to kiss a wrapped present and then she kissed her kitten. Emma sat down on the floor next to her daughter.

"Let Jamie open hers first, and us old people will watch." Daron's dad had leaned back in a chair, his feet propped up on an ottoman. "This is my favorite part of Christmas and it's been a long time since we've celebrated one here at the ranch with a child around."

Jamie didn't have to be told twice. She happily started opening gifts, occasionally pulling her kitten back to her lap when it tried to get away. There were games and books, dolls and a preschool art kit.

Emma watched as Jamie played. She watched and wished that everything could be as perfect as this moment.

Soon, with all the presents opened and the wrapping paper shoved into garbage bags, they all settled down and she knew that it was almost time to talk to Daron.

Art was talking to Daron's dad. His mom and sister were with Emma, clearing the table. Jamie was curled up on a pallet of blankets with a sleeping, purring kitten.

She'd named the kitten Buster.

Yes, it all seemed perfect. But she knew from experience that perfect had a way of falling apart.

Daron walked up behind Emma. She half turned, smiled and went back to drying dishes.

"Walk with me?"

She paused and he thought she might say no. "Okay."

She hung the dish towel on the bar and followed him. He wanted to take her hand, but he had a feeling she wouldn't let him. Not in front of everyone. They walked side by side, not speaking. When they got to the stable, she waited for him to push the door open and she went in ahead of him.

The horses were in stalls. He flipped on lights and she went immediately to them, stopping first at the POA, Pony of America. The small gelding was showy with his Appaloosa markings. He had a nice head and good eyes. For Daron it was always about the eyes.

"This one is too small for you," she said in a soft tone without looking at him. Her hand was on the neck of the pony.

"Yeah, I guess. I just thought someday..." He paused because he didn't know what he'd been thinking, not really. Cart before the horse—that was what had happened that day. Without knowing their future, he had assumed she and Jamie would always be in his life.

Man, he really wanted them in his life.

But he had a bad feeling about this. "Say something."

She put her face to the face of the pony. "He's beautiful."

"Not what I was looking for."

"I know." She moved on to the mare in the next stall. A pretty girl, all showy and expressive.

Daron stepped next to Emma. "Is it because of the kitten?"

She shook her head. He saw a tiny lift of her mouth. "No."

"Are you going to tell me that we're through?"

"What are we, Daron? Friends? Your charity case? We make you feel better about what happened in Afghanistan?" She shook her head. "Forgive me. That was wrong. So wrong."

He shrugged it off. "Maybe those were my intentions at first, to soothe my guilt. I think we both know that. I felt guilty for what happened. And after years of driving past your house, checking on you, it became a habit."

"Right. So how do we know what we really feel? What part of this is habit, what part is real?"

"All I can tell you is what I feel. It's not a secret." He wanted to pull her close, kiss her, tell her she didn't have to be afraid. But he knew that now wasn't the time. She was going to have to figure this out on her own.

He was going to have to let her. He couldn't remember ever having a broken heart. Maybe once, in fifth grade when he had a crush on the art teacher. He'd brought her flowers, written her a poem and she sat him down one day and said someday some girl would come into his life and it would be wonderful. But Miss Craig had a boyfriend and she planned to get married that summer.

He'd been waiting twenty years for that someday girl.

She was standing next to him crying silent tears as she told him, and he shook his head as he listened.

"I think we shouldn't see each other for a while. Because I need to know what I feel. And I need for you to know. I don't want to get six months down the road and realize, or have you realize, that this is wrong. I don't want you to look at me with disgust because I wore the wrong shoes, or fixed my hair the wrong way. I just can't be that person again."

"You aren't that person. You are incredible, strong and independent. I don't care if you go barefoot."

She laughed a little, the sound ending on a sob. "Oh, I think you would. And I would care. If I looked across the table and saw regret in your eyes, I don't know if I could handle that."

"I'm not Andy."

"No, you're not. And I'm trying so hard to not compare. Because it isn't you. It's me. I'm broken. I need to be whole. When I give my heart, I want it to be my whole heart. For the person I love. For my daughter. I want her to know that she has two parents who will love each other, respect each other and stay together for each other and for her."

He kissed the top of her head. "I want that, too. I'm not going to argue with you, but I think we are a good fit. And I think our time together clarifies everything we feel."

"No, because we've been through too much. Not just in the last few weeks but in the last few years."

"Okay, I'm going to give you time. But I want to be very clear about one thing. I know what I feel for you. It isn't pity. It isn't charity. This isn't coming from a guilty conscience."

"But some time apart will help you know for certain."

He drew her to him, touching his mouth to hers, tasting her tears as he kissed her. She clung to him for a moment and then she let go.

"That isn't friendship, Emma."

"I think I should go now."

"If that's what you think you need to do. I…" He shook his head. "No, I don't understand."

"Neither do I," she admitted quietly. "I just feel like this came out of nowhere and I need to know for sure, you need to know, what it is we're feeling."

"And you think we can do that apart?" He shook his head. "Emma, I don't want to be away from you, not even for a day. So I guess I know how I feel."

"Then I'm the one who has to know for sure what you feel, and what I feel. I should go."

"If that's what you want."

He walked her back to the house. She gathered up the stuffed elephant Daron had bought for Jamie, and the games from his parents, the books from his sister. Her granddad had been given a hand-carved checker set. Daron watched as she smiled and talked to his parents, his sister. She stopped to tell Jamie something about her kitten.

He'd forgotten his gift for her. Other than the horses. But he couldn't tell her now that the horses were for her. He handed her a small box. "You can unwrap it later."

She held it for a moment, then tried to give it back.

He shook his head. "It's for you, Emma. It wouldn't suit anyone else and I refuse to take it back."

She put the box in her purse and thanked him. And then she pulled a box from her bag and handed it to him. He opened his gift. A Bible. It was engraved. He opened it and she'd written in the inside that she hoped this Bible would guide him on his journey, wherever it might take him. And she hoped he knew that he had a friend who would always be praying for him.

It sounded like a pretty serious goodbye to him.

Chapter Seventeen

The first day of the New Year dawned cold and rainy. Emma drove out through the field, still in Daron's truck. She had called to tell him she'd sold her steers and was getting her old farm truck fixed. He told her to keep his truck as long as she needed it. He wasn't using it.

He'd asked how she was and she'd told him she was fine. Of course she was fine. And he'd said the same. But she wondered if either of them was truly fine. Fine didn't feel like this, like her world was broken apart and needed to be fitted back together again. Fine didn't feel like waking up every morning wondering if she should call him and tell him she'd made a mistake. Or wondering if he would call and ask to talk.

Or maybe fine was all of those things. And

she wanted more than that. She wanted her world to be beautiful again.

She'd told him she needed time apart. And he was giving her that. Relationships shouldn't be rushed into. She'd made that mistake once before.

She didn't tell him she'd opened his gift, but she should have. She should have thanked him for the bracelet. It was beautiful. And even though she shouldn't, she wore it every day. Because it felt like a piece of him was with her. But then, there was also the kitten. That crazy little feline that followed them around, playing with shoes as they walked, climbing on furniture and terrorizing the dog. It was such an innocent-looking little ball of fur. She smiled at the thought of Buster and how much it was loved by Jamie. And when Jamie talked to her kitten, she talked about Daron.

The cattle came running from the other side of the field. She stopped the truck to drop the round bale, lowering it to the ground with the spike and then pulling away. As the cattle converged on the bale of hay, she got out and grabbed the bag of feed off the back of the truck and carried it to the trough. As she stepped away, the cattle were moving in, nudging and pushing. She climbed back into the truck and headed back to the house.

Granddad normally took care of morning feeding, but he'd been in the kitchen fixing breakfast and she'd needed the fresh air. She needed time alone to think.

Lucy was getting out of her truck as Emma got out to close the gate and latch it. She waved and Lucy headed her way.

"I thought I'd stop by and see how things are going," Lucy said as they walked into the barn, where the lighting was dim and dust danced on the few beams of sunlight.

"I'm good. We'll be going to Austin next week for Jamie's procedure. Did you see your mom?"

Lucy shrugged off the question. "No, but I've seen my partner. Remember him—Daron? He's on a job in Dallas. He looks like someone ran him over with a semi."

Emma headed out the back door of the barn. She fed the chickens, gathered the few eggs and walked back inside. Lucy waited, patiently.

"I'm trying to not hurt him, Lucy. I don't want him confused about what he feels."

Lucy shook her head. "It's really none of my business. I'm the last person who should be giving advice about relationships."

"I don't mind your advice. I just really felt as if everything had moved so quickly and it was wrapped up with Jamie's illness and Pete's addiction. It just needs to be unraveled so we know what we are feeling in each situation."

"That makes sense to me," Lucy agreed. "Can I be there, at the hospital with you?"

"I would love that." She reached for Lucy and pulled her into a stiff hug. "You're not a hugger."

Lucy pulled back. "No, I'm not. I'll forgive you this time."

"Since we're still friends, let's have a cup of coffee and see if Granddad made cinnamon rolls."

"I love that idea."

They were heading to the house when a familiar white truck pulled up. Lucy said something like "uh-oh" and went on inside, leaving Emma in the yard to face Daron.

He got out of his truck, patted her dog, and then he looked at her. She looked at him, too. She wasn't ready to admit how much she missed him.

"Hi."

He pushed back his hat and grinned. "Hey."

"I didn't expect to see you. Lucy said you're in Dallas."

He shrugged off her comment. "I wanted to stop by. I'm home for the day and then back to the job. My mom called. She wanted me to tell you that you and Art are welcome to stay with them when you're in Austin for Jamie's surgery. She insisted, so I told her I'd pass it on."

"That's really nice of her, but she doesn't have to."

"Emma, where are you planning to stay?"

"A hotel. I made reservations."

"Stay with my parents. Please. They'll be upset if you don't. Go the day before the surgery so Jamie can rest up. Stay with them as long as needed. They'll enjoy having you there. My dad says he's going to teach Art to play chess."

She nodded, heat climbing into her cheeks. "Tell them thank you, we appreciate it."

"She's going to be fine." He brushed a hand down her arm, and his fingers touched hers. And then he noticed the bracelet. She saw a hint of a smile. "You opened it. I thought you might not."

"I did, and thank you. It's too much, but I love it."

"Tell Jamie I'll bring her something special to help her recover."

"Not an elephant," Emma warned.

He had started to walk away and he turned, winking as he smiled that slow, easy smile of his. "Not an elephant."

Daron got in his truck, shifted into Reverse, then sat there watching as Emma walked up the steps. She paused on the front porch, but she didn't turn. Pathetic fool that he was, he waited.

After a few minutes he backed out of her drive and headed toward Dallas. Driving away from her was the hardest thing he'd had to do. He had wanted to pull into her house, convince her that what they felt was love and that she should give him a chance. Give *them* a chance.

Instead he'd respected her wishes and hadn't pushed. He could only hope, and pray, that she was heading in the same direction he was. Because the last few days had made things pretty clear for him. She and Jamie meant everything to him.

Boone was waiting for him at their hotel, and also the site of the convention they were providing security for. Daron walked into the room and found his partner sitting on the bed watching a John Wayne movie.

"Pretty stereotypical," Daron said as he pulled a bottle of water out of the fridge.

"What?" Boone reached for his hat and shoved it down on his head. "I think I'm a lot like John Wayne."

"Whatever."

"Did you see her?"

"Yep. I passed on the message from my parents and left. Lucy was there." Daron sat down on the edge of his bed and swigged down half the bottle of water.

"That's an odd pair, Lucy and Emma."

Daron shrugged. "Not really. Makes sense to me that they'd be friends."

"Yeah, I guess. But have you ever known Lucy to have a friend, other than us two?"

Daron clicked off the TV.

"What are you going to do now?"

"My job. I've been distracted for the past month, and distraction can get a guy killed."

"Yeah, it can."

They both went to a dark place. Daron guessed it was the same dark place. A place where he'd been fooled by feelings for a woman and because of it he'd led a few guys into danger. And one of them had died.

Chapter Eighteen

~

Emma tried to pretend it was any other morning. For Jamie's sake. For her own. But it wasn't. They weren't at home; they were in Austin staying with Daron's parents. And even though Jamie was too young to understand what was happening, she had an idea that it was a big day. She'd been fussy for a few days. She'd cried last night that she wanted Daron.

That had taken Emma by surprise. Jamie always wanted her mommy. Sometimes she wanted Art. But last night she'd wanted the person who had been their rock during a difficult time.

Emma had to admit, she missed him, too.

His parents were wonderful. They were kind and caring. They loved their son. They might interfere in his life and want something different from him, something other than the career he'd chosen. But they were good people.

Emma turned on the lamp. It was still dark outside, but she could hear people stirring. Daron's parents insisted on going with her to the hospital. Granddad, of course, would be with her. He was always with her. He was her rock. She wouldn't forget that. He'd been wiping her tears and cleaning up her messes for a long time.

Her granddad had taught her what a real man was and how he should treat a woman. He'd been everything to her: a mom, a dad and a grandfather.

Jamie huddled on the bed in her robe. "I want cereal."

"No cereal this morning, sweetie. Later you can eat."

"I'm hungry."

Emma gathered her daughter up. "I know, honey. I promise you'll get to eat. Just not right now."

Jamie sobbed against her shoulder. "Mommy. Please."

"Soon. And you're going to feel so much better. You're going to run. And you're going to chase the kitten."

"I can run fast."

"Yes, you'll run even faster." And not be tired after playing. She wouldn't need to catch her breath after chasing her kitten.

Two hours later the nurse escorted Emma, Art and the McKays to a surgical waiting room where they would be given updates. The pediatric cardiologist had explained the process of threading the catheter through the vein in Jamie's neck to fix the hole in the ventricular septum. He explained the possible problems and what they would do if any of those problems occurred.

Emma sat by the window and prayed. She prayed for her daughter, for the surgeons, the nurses, the anesthesiologist. The door to the waiting room opened.

The Shaws, Andy's parents, stepped in. Mrs. Shaw looked unsure. "We wanted to be here, for you and for her. Is that okay? We understand if you don't want us."

"No, please stay." Emma wiped at her eyes. Silly, useless tears. "The procedure just started. It could be several hours."

"Can we get you anything?" Mr. Shaw asked.

"I'm fine," Emma answered. Then she let the rest of them talk in soft whispers, about Jamie, about the weather and about politics. She watched the clock. The minutes ticked by so slowly. Her heartbeat caught the rhythm of the clock. Each tick, each heartbeat, one step closer.

The door opened again. Her heart did a funny catch. She turned, hoping, expecting. Wanting Daron. It was a nurse, smiling at all of them.

"I wanted to update you. We're halfway there. She's doing great. The doctor said he doesn't foresee any problems at this point."

Emma blinked back more tears. She nodded and thanked the nurse, who slipped quietly out of the room.

She wanted to call Daron. She wanted him to know that Jamie was doing well. Of course they'd known she would. She thought about how different it would have felt had he been here. She was surrounded by people, but she felt alone. If Daron had been here, she wouldn't have felt alone.

He was her partner. He'd become her partner the day he stepped into her hospital room after Jamie was born. He'd brought flowers and told her he would always be there if she needed anything.

She'd sent him away. Now she was in the wilderness alone. She closed her eyes and took a deep breath. No, not alone. It was almost as if God was speaking to her heart.

She wasn't alone. He had this. He had a plan.
He had the path before her and He would be
her light.

The nurse returned a little over an hour
later. "We're all finished. She did great and
she'll soon be moved to a room."

Emma stood. She couldn't sit. She had
to hug someone, so she hugged the nurse.
"Thank you."

The nurse returned the hug. "You're so welcome. She did the hard work. Jamie and Dr.
Lee."

The nurse left. Emma stood in the center
of the room surrounded by people she hadn't
expected to have in her life. Granddad, of
course. Andy's parents, though, they were a
surprise. She accepted their hugs and well-
wishes.

"We're going to go now," Mr. Shaw told
her. "Can we visit tomorrow?"

"Of course you can." She hugged her ex-
mother-in-law again. "Jamie will like that."

After they left she hugged Daron's parents. "Thank you for being here with us. And
for letting us stay with you. It has meant so
much."

Nora McKay held her in a tight hug. "Of
course we wanted you with us. And I know

Daron wanted to be here. He's been working in Dallas."

"I know." She walked away, back to her window.

"Should someone call Daron?" she said, without looking back at his parents. It was easier to sit facing the window. That way, she didn't see their concern. She didn't have to make conversation.

"What if I just show up?" The voice, low, so sweetly familiar that it almost undid her.

She flew out of the chair. He was standing in the doorway, his hair a mess, a suit with the tie loose around his neck and the jacket unbuttoned.

"You're here."

"Yes, I'm here. I had to be here."

She wanted to touch him, but they had an audience, a very interested audience. She focused on the tie, hanging loose around his neck. She straightened it a bit and smoothed down his collar. "I'm glad you're here."

She caught his gaze and held it. "I've missed you."

"I've missed you, too." He exhaled, then pulled her close. "I hope you understand what this has been like for me. I hope, and I mean this with love, that you've been just as miserable."

"I have. I really have."

The door opened again. The nurse smiled at them all. "Mom, do you want to come down and see your little girl?"

"Yes, please." More than anything. "Can Daron come with me? She'll want to see him."

"Is he family?" the nurse asked, still standing in the doorway.

"He's my best friend."

The nurse smiled. "I think we can allow a best friend today. Especially if it will make our patient happy. Before the anesthesia hit she was telling me about a kitten and a guy named Daron that her mommy loves."

Emma felt heat crawl into her cheeks.

"You love me?" Daron whispered as they walked down the hall.

She didn't answer.

At the door to the cardiac intensive-care unit, the nurse stopped them. "We have her in here for now, just to monitor her and make sure all her vitals are strong. We'll probably move her to a regular room in the morning. I'd like for you both to scrub hands and arms and put on a gown, and let's limit the visit to five or ten minutes right now. We'll need to do some work with her and she's going to be tired. But I promise in about thirty minutes or so we'll come back and get you for a longer visit."

"Thank you." Emma moved to the sink the nurse had indicated. She scrubbed her hands and arms.

Daron waited until she finished and was gowning up before he stepped forward to wash. She held a gown out and he slipped into it. Hand in hand, they walked through the doors into that brightly lit and sterile world.

When Emma spotted her daughter, she wanted to cry. She wanted to pick her up and hold her. But she couldn't. There were tubes, monitors, IVs. She looked so small and fragile in the hospital bed, surrounded by equipment, monitored, watched by a nurse.

"She's going to be fine," Daron said. "She's strong and she has a mommy who's tough."

She leaned into him. "Yes, she's going to be fine."

Jamie opened her eyes, then opened them wider when she saw Daron. She smiled, just a tiny smile but it was her smile. She whispered, "Mommy?"

Emma kissed her cheek. "Mommy is here. And Daron came to see you, too. We love you."

We. She didn't know that they were a "we,"

but it felt right for the moment. They could be a "we" when it came to Jamie. The two of them were both there for her.

She sat in the chair next to her daughter's bed and held her hand until she fell asleep. Daron had slipped away, telling her he would meet her in the chapel.

When the nurse told her she'd have to leave for a bit, Emma kissed Jamie again and slipped from the room as her daughter slept.

Where was the chapel? She vaguely remembered seeing a small prayer room near the surgical waiting room. She headed that way. When she got there she peeked in and she saw Daron at the window. His head was bowed. She waited and finally he turned.

He had flowers and balloons.

"I don't know if they'll let her have flowers," she said.

"They're for you." He looked up at the balloons with the words Get Well Soon printed on them, and he grinned. "It's all they had in the hospital gift shop."

Daron looked awkward with the bouquet. He handed them to her and she took them, looking up at the balloon with the get-well message.

"I know you need time," he started, pushing a hand through his hair. "But I don't," he said next. "I don't need time to know that I love you. I love Jamie. Every moment since Christmas, I've missed you. You are my life, Emma. You are my next breath. Good grief, you have me spouting poetry. I know this is not the best time. I know you're worried about Jamie. But I can't do this life thing without you."

"Get well soon?" She looked up at the balloon and laughed.

"You'll never forget this moment," he assured her with that dimple showing in his cheek. He settled a hand on her waist and pulled her close.

"No, I guess I won't." She leaned close, breathing him in, wishing he would kiss her.

"I don't want time to think. I want time with you. Let's just pretend that balloon says something totally different."

She felt lighter than she'd felt in days. A giggle erupted and she touched his cheek. "What does the balloon say?"

He dropped to one knee and she couldn't breathe. The room spun in a crazy way and he smiled up at her. "The balloon says I love you and I plan to love you more each and every day. I want to have a family with you. I want to grow old with you. Will you marry me?"

Tears began to fall and she laughed through the haze of moisture. "We'll need a bigger balloon."

"This is not a moment when you want to tease a man." He was still on one knee. "I just poured my heart out to you. Don't leave me hanging. Or kneeling, as the case may be."

She put the flowers on the table next to them and leaned to cup his cheeks and kiss him.

Daron stood up, holding her hands in his. She'd kissed him. That meant he probably ought to kiss her back.

"Will." He kissed her. "You." He kissed her again. "Marry." And again. "Me?"

And then he settled his lips on hers, kissing her the way he'd wanted to since she walked into this room. He kissed her until he hoped her knees were weak, and so was her resolve to resist him.

When he pulled back she was clinging to his arms. "Please answer me."

"I can't. You keep kissing me," she said.

For that he kissed her again. Her lips were sweet beneath his, and her hands held tight to his shoulders.

This time when he pulled away from her, she nodded.

"Yes, I think I will marry you."

He picked her up and swung her around the small room. Her foot hit the flowers and he caught them before they could hit the floor.

"I love you."

"I love you, too." She wrapped her arms around his neck and held on as he scooped her up. He grabbed the flowers and put them in her hands, then carried her back to the waiting room.

As they stepped through the door, everyone inside stood and applauded. His parents. Art. They all looked pretty pleased.

"I guess I don't need to announce that I'm the happiest man in the world?" Daron asked as he set Emma on her feet next to him.

"I think we were all just waiting for the two of you to figure things out," Art said. "Good thing, because I was tired of waiting. I'd just like to tell you, I hope you've got an in-law room in that big house of yours."

"Art, we have plenty of room for you."

The door opened again and the nurse peeked in. "I'm glad you all are celebrating. Our little patient would like some company."

Daron walked down the hall at Emma's side. Always at her side. That was where he planned to stay. Forever.

Epilogue

April was the perfect month for a wedding in Texas. The reason was simple: the bluebonnets were blooming. Nothing was more beautiful than Texas Hill Country in spring.

She also chose to get married in the country church where Remington Jenkins was pastor. The church was situated in a valley with fields of wildflowers spreading out from it like deep purple carpet. It was as if God was the florist for her wedding.

"Are you almost ready?" Lucy stepped into the room wearing a black evening dress.

She wasn't a bridesmaid. The bridesmaids wore dresses the color of spring. No, she was one of the groomsmen. She and Boone. Oregon and Lily were the matron of honor and bridesmaid. Oregon wore a pale lavender dress. Lily's dress was pale yellow. The bouquets were filled with wildflowers in shades of yellow, purple and white.

Jamie was her flower girl. Her blond hair in ringlets and a wreath of baby's breath atop her little head. She carried a basket of flower petals that she would sprinkle along the aisle of the church. If the petals survived. At the moment she had several of them lined up on the windowsill and she was arranging them like little flowers.

"I'm almost ready." Emma looked into the mirror. She hadn't known until recently that her grandmother's wedding dress, the same wedding dress the Lewis women had worn for three generations, was in a box in Art's closet. He'd had it sealed, in case she should ever want it.

He hadn't told her before. She didn't ask why.

Oregon stepped forward to adjust her veil.

"You look beautiful," Oregon said softly, a shimmer of tears in her eyes. "I'm going to cry."

Lily groaned. "I don't get that. It's a wedding. It's a happy time. I think when I get married, I'll elope."

"Don't you dare," all three of the women said in unison.

"I should go check on the groom," Lucy

said as she opened the door. "He's a little bit nervous. He actually sent me in here to make sure you didn't duck out the back. I think Boone made him watch the movie *Runaway Bride.*"

"Tell him I'm not going anywhere."

"Except down the aisle," Oregon added. "And tell him she loves him."

"Yes, I love him." She loved him so much it hurt.

The next person to pound on the door was Granddad. Oregon let him in. "My goodness, you are beautiful, Em."

"Granddad, have I told you how much I love you?"

"I love you back." He took her hand and slipped a pretty ring on the finger of her right hand. "I want you to have this. It was your mom's. Now, don't cry. Something borrowed, something blue, something old and something new. I guess I said that wrong, but I'm close. That ring is old. I believe it was my grandmother's. And now it's yours. But I'm also giving you something new."

"And what's that?"

"New hope and a new beginning." He grinned. "Now, that's something not everyone can give their girl. But you deserve it and I'm glad you stopped being afraid to accept it."

"Me, too, Art. Me, too." She hugged him tight. "I think it's time."

"Yes, I believe it is. Do you like my new bibs?"

She laughed and dabbed at her eyes with the tissue Oregon pushed into her hand. Art preened a bit in his dark blue bib overalls beneath a sport coat.

"I wouldn't have you any other way. You look very handsome."

"I thought so. I even let Allie at the Clip and Curl trim my hair and give me a shave. I kind of liked that." He rubbed his hand across his very smooth cheek.

He crossed the room to Jamie, kissed her cheek and told her she was as pretty as a field of wildflowers.

Oregon peeked into the hall. "It's time."

She opened the door wide. She went first down the hallway and Lily followed. Jamie walked in front of Emma and her grandfather. Emma put her hand on Art's arm and they took their time walking down the dimly lit hall to the outside door. They walked out into fresh air and she breathed deep as Art guided her up the front steps of the church. Jamie waited for them at the top of the steps. She had a flower petal on top of her head and she was grinning as if she might be up to something.

Music was playing. Someone was singing. Emma had picked the song and now she couldn't remember which one. She could only think of one thing—Daron. After today they would be married. She, Daron and Jamie would be a family. And Granddad. She smiled up at her grandfather.

"Here we go, kiddo." He smiled down at her. "I sure love you and I'm sorry that life has been hard, but you've been a blessing to an old man. And I hope this young man is a blessing to you."

"Granddad, I'm going to look terrible if you make me cry. My nose will be red and mascara will run down my cheeks. But I love you, too."

They both laughed a little. Jamie glanced back at them and Emma nodded, indicating her daughter should take her walk down the aisle.

Emma looked toward the front of the church. Lily and Oregon were on the left, smiling, holding their bouquets. Boone and Lucy stood on the opposite side. And next to them, Daron. He wore a Western-cut tuxedo. His hair had been trimmed. Her heart filled to overflowing because he caught her eye and then he smiled at Jamie, encouraging her. She sprinkled flowers as Art and Emma started down the aisle.

As they got to the front of the church, Jamie turned and with that mischievous grin she picked up the basket and tossed flowers in the air. Wildflower petals fluttered around Emma as Art released her and she stepped to Daron's side.

Remington smiled at them, at the wedding party, and then he began. "You may be seated. Who gives this bride in marriage?"

Her granddad stood nearby, chest puffed out in pride. "Me and the Good Lord."

The guests laughed a little. Granddad winked and took his seat.

Emma wanted to remember every word, every moment of the ceremony. But later what she remembered most was her hand in Daron's and Jamie at her side. And it felt right. It felt like they were a family.

She looked up at the man who would be her husband and he gave her a slow wink and that steady, easy smile of his. He placed the ring on her finger and she placed one on his. And then he kissed her with Jamie standing between them, hugging both their legs.

With the crowd cheering, he lifted Jamie and took Emma by the hand, and they walked back down the aisle with wildflower petals floating through the air and a song being played. She thought it might have been "Can I Have This Dance?"

She only remembered that it felt so right to stand next to Daron and know that now and forever he would be hers and she would be his. And maybe in a year or two Jamie would have a little brother or sister.

Yes, her heart was full to overflowing. And God had indeed blessed her with this second chance.

* * * * *

If you loved this story, pick up these other
MARTIN'S CROSSING *books,*

HER RANCHER BODYGUARD
THE RANCHER'S FIRST LOVE
THE RANCHER'S SECOND CHANCE
THE RANCHER TAKES A BRIDE
A RANCHER FOR CHRISTMAS

from bestselling author
Brenda Minton

Available now from Love Inspired!

Find more great reads at
www.LoveInspired.com

Dear Reader,

I'm so thrilled that you've joined me for another visit to Martin's Crossing! *Her Guardian Rancher* brings familiar faces and new characters. Daron McKay has been a favorite character of mine and it seems fitting that the Martin's Crossing series should end with his story. Emma Shaw is an amazing heroine, and in her, Daron will find a lasting love. Together with her daughter, Jamie, the three create an amazing family and a story I hope you will love!

Blessings!
Brenda

REQUEST YOUR FREE BOOKS!

2 FREE RIVETING INSPIRATIONAL NOVELS
PLUS 2 FREE MYSTERY GIFTS

Love Inspired.
SUSPENSE
RIVETING INSPIRATIONAL ROMANCE

YES! Please send me 2 FREE Love Inspired® Suspense novels and my 2 FREE mystery gifts (gifts are worth about $10). After receiving them, if I don't wish to receive any more books, I can return the shipping statement marked "cancel." If I don't cancel, I will receive 4 brand-new novels every month and be billed just $4.99 per book in the U.S. or $5.49 per book in Canada. That's a savings of at least 17% off the cover price. It's quite a bargain! Shipping and handling is just 50¢ per book in the U.S. and 75¢ per book in Canada.* I understand that accepting the 2 free books and gifts places me under no obligation to buy anything. I can always return a shipment and cancel at any time. Even if I never buy another book, the two free books and gifts are mine to keep forever.

123/323 IDN GH5Z

Name	(PLEASE PRINT)	
Address		Apt. #
City	State/Prov.	Zip/Postal Code

Signature (if under 18, a parent or guardian must sign)

Mail to the **Reader Service:**
IN U.S.A.: P.O. Box 1867, Buffalo, NY 14240-1867
IN CANADA: P.O. Box 609, Fort Erie, Ontario L2A 5X3

**Are you a current subscriber to Love Inspired® Suspense books
and want to receive the larger-print edition?
Call 1-800-873-8635 or visit www.ReaderService.com.**

* Terms and prices subject to change without notice. Prices do not include applicable taxes. Sales tax applicable in N.Y. Canadian residents will be charged applicable taxes. Offer not valid in Quebec. This offer is limited to one order per household. Not valid for current subscribers to Love Inspired Suspense books. All orders subject to credit approval. Credit or debit balances in a customer's account(s) may be offset by any other outstanding balance owed by or to the customer. Please allow 4 to 6 weeks for delivery. Offer available while quantities last.

> **Your Privacy**—The Reader Service is committed to protecting your privacy. Our Privacy Policy is available online at www.ReaderService.com or upon request from the Reader Service.
> We make a portion of our mailing list available to reputable third parties that offer products we believe may interest you. If you prefer that we not exchange your name with third parties, or if you wish to clarify or modify your communication preferences, please visit us at www.ReaderService.com/consumerchoice or write to us at Reader Service Preference Service, P.O. Box 9062, Buffalo, NY 14240-9062. Include your complete name and address.

YES! Please send me **The Western Promises Collection** in Larger Print. This collection begins with 3 FREE books and 2 FREE gifts (gifts valued at approx. $14.00 retail) in the first shipment, along with the other first 4 books from the collection! If I do not cancel, I will receive 8 monthly shipments until I have the entire 51-book Western Promises collection. I will receive 2 or 3 FREE books in each shipment and I will pay just $4.99 US/ $5.89 CDN for each of the other four books in each shipment, plus $2.99 for shipping and handling per shipment. *If I decide to keep the entire collection, I'll have paid for only 32 books, because 19 books are FREE! I understand that accepting the 3 free books and gifts places me under no obligation to buy anything. I can always return a shipment and cancel at any time. My free books and gifts are mine to keep no matter what I decide.

272 HCN 3070 472 HCN 3070

Name	(PLEASE PRINT)	
Address		Apt. #
City	State/Prov.	Zip/Postal Code

Signature (if under 18, a parent or guardian must sign)

Mail to the **Reader Service:**

IN U.S.A.: P.O. Box 1867, Buffalo, NY 14240-1867
IN CANADA: P.O. Box 609, Fort Erie, Ontario L2A 5X3

* Terms and prices subject to change without notice. Prices do not include applicable taxes. Sales tax applicable in N.Y. Canadian residents will be charged applicable taxes. This offer is limited to one order per household. All orders subject to approval. Credit or debit balances in a customer's account(s) may be offset by any other outstanding balance owed by or to the customer. Please allow 4 to 6 weeks for delivery. Offer available while quantities last. Offer not available to Quebec residents.

Your Privacy—The Reader Service is committed to protecting your privacy. Our Privacy Policy is available online at www.ReaderService.com or upon request from the Reader Service.

We make a portion of our mailing list available to reputable third parties that offer products we believe may interest you. If you prefer that we not exchange your name with third parties, or if you wish to clarify or modify your communication preferences, please visit us at www.ReaderService.com/consumerschoice or write to us at Reader Service Preference Service, P.O. Box 9062, Buffalo, NY 14240-9062. Include your complete name and address.